PICTURE FRAME

PICTURE FRAME

by

LYNTON LAMB

LONDON
VICTOR GOLLANCZ LTD
1972

© Lynton Lamb 1972

ISBN 0 575 01440 7

PRINTED IN GREAT BRITAIN
BY EBENEZER BAYLIS & SON LIMITED
THE TRINITY PRESS, WORCESTER, AND LONDON

The 'Stour Siblings' can only be found in my imaginary 'Soke of Domcaister'; so no identification should be attempted with actual places or institutions. Certainly the meagre 'Saint Osyth Sibling' has nothing to do with the Essex St Osyth, its priory, parish life or martello towers.

Overleaf is a list of the fictional characters. They are not identifiable with any living persons. However, some actual painters are mentioned, none of whom is alive. These are:

Bernardo Bitti (c. 1548–1610)
Eugène Delacroix (1798–1863)
Pierre Auguste Renoir (1841–1919)
John Singer Sargent (1856–1925)
Pierre Bonnard (1867–1947)
Edouard Vuillard (1868–1940)
Raoul Dufy (1877–1953)
Alfred Munnings (1878–1950)
Giorgio Morandi (1890–1964)
Mark Rothko (1903–1970)

MAIN CHARACTERS

The Revd Frank Fenwick, M.C., M.A., a rural dean &c
Penelope Fenwick, his wife
The Revd Martin Chew, incumbent at Saint Osyth Sibling
Martha Chew, his wife
Mostyn Pringle, a bird-watcher
Thomas Pringle, his grandson
Jack Sherard, cousin to Thomas Pringle
Margaret Capper, an actress
Rowland Mallender, of the Cornford Gallery, London
Judith Ramage, his secretary-assistant
Lord Culvert of Channel, a shareholder in the gallery
Cyprian Gradual, a lawyer
Gregory Poleyn, an architect
Bulmer Bestworth, a printer
Jimmy Bestworth, his son
Clara Neame, a publican's wife
Johnny Plumb, her brother
Janice Tyler, a postwoman
Charley Gotobed, an Autolycus of sorts
Matilda Prosit, a Chelsea landlady

Detective Chief Superintendent Quill,
Detective Inspector Charles Glover, } Stourminster C.I.D.
Detective Sergeant Simmons,

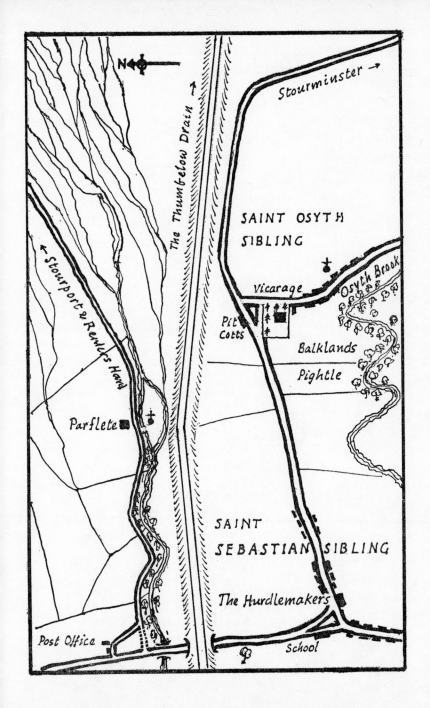

'WELL, MY DEAR,' said the Reverend Frank Fenwick as he sat down to luncheon, 'there's now a distinguished painter at Saint Sebastian Sibling.'

'Good heavens!' said Mrs Fenwick, 'he must be mad!'

'Oh? Can no good thing come into the Stour Siblings? I am told that the old church schools at Saint Sebastian are being "used as a studio by a Mr Sherard from London". Furthermore, he has a "very oddly-coloured van" ... Jack Sherard, wouldn't you say?'

'But, my dear Frank, Jack is no *landscape* painter. He is to be the new Mark Rothko. He won't need to paint real live earth. I imagine there's precious little of anything else there. And I can't suppose Meg Capper will consent to hold his hand in the school-marm's house at Saint Seb.'

'Oh, does that still go on? He always seemed a cold fish to me.'

Mrs Fenwick gave him what Jane Austen calls a 'conscious' look. Before she had given up her work as a stage-designer to become a parson's wife, they both used to see a lot of Margaret Capper, the actress, whom they had met while *The Prickly Pear* was in production. The play had made many post-war reputations and given Margaret Capper her first important part. Hugh Capper, her husband, had been a somewhat discredited actor. He had died on an ENSA tour in 1945; and she later became semi-attached to the recently demobilised Jack Sherard. But she did not re-marry.

Managements had begun to offer the kind of plays that suited her.

'Surely, Frank,' Penelope Fenwick now said, 'there is no one left at Saint Seb other than the Chews at their wet, wet vicarage—oh, and the brent geese, of course.'

'That's not quite right, my dear. The Chews are now at Saint Osyth; and I don't think brent geese would come so far above high tide as any of the Sebastian islands. There may be some barnacle geese there . . . '

She wrinkled her nose at him; but he continued, 'There is even a shop and a sub-post office at Saint Sebastian. I don't suppose either does much business. However, there does happen to be one big house there: not an old one, of course. It's a sort of Edwardian "Maple Grove". But I see clearly that you won't accept any such architecturally mixed periods. And quite right too.'

'Thank you, Frank. We had better not confuse *Emma* and *The Forsyte Saga*. Were you not thinking of "Mapledurham"? Was this house of yours built by a "young Bosinney"?'

'I expect I have got it wrong. It certainly is not stone-faced *art nouveau* or anything like that. Red brick with tile-hung gables and a lot of white paintwork. All on its own near what is left of the church.'

'What's "left"? Bare ruined choirs?'

'Not as bad as that! But the church is now closed and will have to be made redundant. I must go out there. For one thing there is a painting the Sibthorps gave.'

She said that she particularly mistrusted the Sibthorps when they came bearing gifts.*

'Oh, this would have been in the eighteenth century. Chew, the vicar, knows nothing about it as yet. He has not even an Inventory or Terrier of the parish.'

*Death of a Dissenter.

12

She looked holier-than-thou. '"Most unfortunate. It is *un*-deniably most un-*four*-chinnit".'

'Well, quite apart from this painting or whatever it may turn out to be, it looks as if I must go there and poke about among disembowelled hassocks, poppyhead finials and plastered-over piscinas for anything the archdeacon can find a place for elsewhere.'

'My poor dear Frank, surely someone can be found to help you?'

'Well, we shall see. I am sorry to say it, but I think I could get on a deal quicker without Mr Chew, whose church it is. Squints, stoups and riddels are all riddles to him: just quaint relics of the dear olden time.'

The Reverend Frank Fenwick, M.C., M.A., was the rector of Fleury Feverel with Hallam, and an honorary Canon of Stourminster Cathedral. He was also (and hence the subject of conversation) Rural Dean of the Stour Siblings, in the seaward corner of which were the five squat steeples of Saint Cedd, Saint Edmund, Saint Felix, Saint Osyth and Saint Sebastian Sibling. At Saint Sebastian, open cornlands gave place to eyots and water meadows. In these gusty haunts of coot and hern lingered a few morose descendants of wherry-men and reed-thatchers. And why, he wondered, should an extremely sophisticated exponent of abstract expressionism decide to set up his easel in the redundant schoolrooms of this rural slum?

* * *

The Reverend Martin Chew, vicar of the parishes of Saints Osyth and Sebastian Sibling, was unexpectedly puzzled as he reached for the knocker on the door of the old school house. He had just seen the odd-looking van that was standing outside. Since it had originally been intended to carry plate-glass it was tall for its width. But its oddness was due to the fact that its sides had been painted with irregular bands of colour so alike in tone that it was hard to determine, he thought, where one colour ended and the next began. Neat, he supposed, searching instinctively for a cliché, neat but not gaudy.

Perhaps it was a trick of the light? He looked up. The sky, although unclouded, was beginning to lose its brightness. But it was still daylight, with a promise, he decided, pleased to have placed it, of a beauteous evening calm and free. His upraised hand groped but failed to find the knocker.

'This will never do,' he muttered, shaking his head. Then, in ringing tones, '"Ye men of Galilee, why stand ye gazing up into heaven?"'

The door at this moment swung open, and a tall middle-aged man said, 'I beg your pardon, sir. I did not realise that there was anyone here. I hope you have not been kept waiting?'

'No, indeed, Mr er . . . only this very moment. It *is* Mr Sherard, isn't it?'

The stranger bowed.

'Just so,' said the vicar.

There was a pause, and then, from somewhere within, a low-pitched woman's voice said very clearly, '"Thou art such a tedious lady; and thy breath smells of lemon peels . . ."' The vicar, who knew the building, judged that this sibylline utterance came from one of the old school rooms.

'*The Duchess of Malfi*,' said Mr Sherard, 'and may I take it that you are the vicar, sir?'

'My name is Chew, Mr Sherard, Martin Chew. I hope I do not intrude? I am vicar here, certainly. I had heard that you had come among us from London. Um? Is that correct? This is a long way from Piccadilly, as the song says. Our rural dean, whom you may know—his wife is very artistic—said that you were an artist.'

His pale prominent eyes, like gooseberries, doubtfully took in the neatness of Mr Sherard, his well-creased trousers, his clean blue cotton shirt, his expensive-looking shoes.

'I am a painter, yes,' said Mr Sherard.

'Oh, that is good, very good! Excellent, indeed. Ah . . . we are country-folk here, you will find . . . we are unused, quite unused . . . but I fear that this is not a picturesque district . . . I hope there may be something to catch your eye . . . may I ask, do you, er, work with models, Mr Sherard?'

'Well, no, vicar. I am not a figurative painter. Not even portraits . . . but perhaps you will come in, sir? I have finished for the day; but I think there will be light enough if you would care to see what is going on.'

'Oh, thank you, thank you. You are very kind. I hope I am not . . . but since you suggest it, I should be very . . . I am, need I say? a total . . . quite a tyro . . . however . . . dear me . . . ah, well! After you, by your leave . . . of course, I remember the school we used . . . thank you, thank you.'

The light was excellent. What had been the two big school rooms, with a folded-back partition between, had a tall window at the end of each. The match-boarded walls and ceiling had been freshly painted a pleasant pale green. The place felt clean and airy: indeed, cleaner than Mr Chew remembered from the days when he had been a school-visitor.

There was a large, somewhat paint-stained deal table with a carefully wiped glass top. A row of what looked like house-painter's brushes hung bristle-down; and large tins of house-hold emulsion-paint were on a shelf.

Many unframed canvases were propped against the walls. They were darkly painted in bands of colour; and from their enigmatic surfaces hung random strips of tape. The vicar asked what these attachments were supposed to represent;

but it was explained to him that adhesive tape was used for temporary masking-out so that a colour could be given a straight, hard edge. The vicar said that he was surprised that this should be 'allowed' since he thought that the ability to colour-in freehand without going over the edges was an essential pre-qualification for an artist. Getting no answer, he stooped to examine a work that seemed to be black all over; or if not entirely black, then with a few patches on it of less intense darkness. As he moved along, he realised that most of the paintings, like the side of the van outside, held colours of almost identical tone. Sometimes the divisions were hard and straight; sometimes they roughly overlapped. He sighed, as one getting a dusty answer when in search of consistency.

A door from the yard opened and a lady came in with a roll of typescript. She was undeniably handsome, with short dark hair, but slightly stooping and haggard-looking. She wore what seemed to be a black track-suit. She apologised in a resonant contralto for interrupting them.

The vicar, relieved from art-appreciation, hastened to say, 'Not at all, not at all! It is I who have intruded on you both at this busy time. I must take myself off, Mrs Sherard.'

Jack Sherard thereupon said, 'Meg, my dear, let me introduce the Reverend Martin Chew. Mr Chew, Mrs Margaret Capper.'

There was a silence. The vicar made a bob towards the lady and then said, 'Please tell me, Mr Sherard, what do you mean to do with these, with these, er, works of yours. Um?'

'I am getting them ready, vicar, for a retrospective exhibition I am to have at the Whitechapel Gallery.'

'Whitechapel, in London, um? Well, perhaps you will one day exhibit nearer the West End, um? The Royal Academy, um?'

Mrs Capper, who was a mistress of exits, returned to the yard, whence she was soon heard to be duchess still. The vicar asked whether living-accommodation at the school-house was not a trifle cramped.

'I am staying at the Crown and Cresset, vicar, in Stour-minster. You see, I have lost my studio in Hammersmith: it is to be pulled down to make way for a ring road; so I must find another. Meanwhile my cousin, Thomas Pringle, kindly offered me this place until my show. It is proving very convenient.'

'Ah! How very interesting! So Mr Pringle is your cousin? He is a comparative new-comer to us in the Siblings. We had been wondering what plans he may have had for settling here. There have been rumours, disturbing to some I could name, that he intends to open another shop. Small profits and slow returns, I fear . . . '

'I wouldn't know. But he was at this school as a boy.'

'Mr Pringle? You do surprise me! Well, indeed! How very interesting! That certainly may explain . . . This is the Return of the Native, um? . . . There has also been some, er, speculation as to his apparent departure. Ha! a contradic-tion in terms! Where is he now? Apart from the expected pleasure of making your, um, acquaintance, I did rather hope that you might be able to tell me whether you had heard from him recently.'

'No, vicar. I have seen nothing of him since the day in London when he arranged for me to come here. He was to have let me in, and I had written to confirm the approximate time of my arrival. There was no sign of him when I drove up. I asked at the pub across the Green—the Hurdlemakers, isn't it? But the landlord's wife seemed barely civil. I could get no help from any one.'

'Alas, sir, I am sorry to say that natives of these parts were described as "a bold, artful, surly, savage race". But I interrupted you.'

'Oh, I eventually found the key under a mat. The place was in some disorder. Even in the bedroom that he had been using cupboards had been emptied and pulled out from the wall. But I have still heard nothing from him after all these weeks.'

'Um! Is he also an artist?'

'Good lord, no! He's a surveyor, or something like that. He works in London, or did. He may have intended to settle here.'

'Did he sketch at all, as an amateur, I mean?'

'I should not think so, vicar. I never heard of it. But I don't know him well. Our families were not brought up together. So I was surprised—and grateful—for his offer of this place. My forthcoming show at the Whitechapel was not general news; but *he* seemed to have heard of it, although I don't think he was interested in the exhibition world, let alone in the sort of work I do.'

'Ahem! I too am out of my depth there, as you will, no doubt, have gathered. But the last time that I actually saw your cousin was at my vicarage in Saint Osyth. It was then I heard that you were coming. But he brought me a picture! You are surprised? He asked me to look after this for a while. To keep this, um, work for him at the vicarage, in fact.'

'Was it valuable, did he say?'

'Well, now, that is the, um, point of my asking . . . I certainly would not have wanted the responsibility if . . . But I must confess that my wife and I think it a terrible daub. It's an oil painting, I should imagine. A sketch of some ladies in a garden. But I assure you it is nothing that we could suppose valuable, um? It is no Sargent, or anything like that! Oh, dear me, no! For one thing there are bits of white canvas left on the faces and dresses and round the edges of things. I suppose it's unfinished. The canvas is just roughly tacked to a sheet of cardboard. We have put it in our attic.

I don't think it can come to any harm there. But seeing that you are related to Mr Pringle . . . and he said that he only wanted me to look after it for two or three days . . . and that was several weeks ago . . . I wonder, would you care to see it, Mr Sherard?'

'Certainly, vicar, if you think I can help. Mrs Capper has to get a London train from Stourminster, but I am sure she won't mind if I stop at your vicarage on the way.'

When they reached Saint Osyth Sibling, Margaret Capper excused herself and remained in the car with the script of *The Duchess of Malfi*. Meanwhile, with some bowing and backing over precedence, Jack Sherard was shown up the vicarage staircase. In the lumber room a canvas loosely attached to Essex board was leaning against a wall between a rocking horse and a mangle.

'My God!' said Jack Sherard, 'it's a Vuillard!'

II

SHORTLY BEFORE the battle of the Falaise gap in Normandy, 063191 J. S. Sherard, Captain, R.E., had been at Corps headquarters. He shared an office truck with one Woozy Watkins, late of Wardour Street, and had decided that he would not be sorry to get away from the reminiscences of that officer, who, like Horace of old, believed himself to have been acceptable to the girls and to have striven among them not without mention in dispatches.

Captain Sherard, therefore, was glad to have been sent elsewhere. More information had been needed for training purposes about ground-to-ground observation in well-wooded country; and the captain, who had been on a camouflage course, had been accordingly attached for this purpose to a divisional headquarters in the *bocage*. In the way of his new duties at this headquarters he had been asked by the gunners to report on one of their observation posts.

'Of course,' he was told, 'we may up-sticks any moment. But our man there is a bit jittery, poor sod. Gerry goes on plastering a house a bit to his left. Gerry's no fool, but we don't think our o.p. has been rumbled. If you will produce your little atlas, old boy, we'll show you where it is. But for God's sake don't go marking the bloody talc in case you get put in the bag. Here we go. This Bois Mesnil is the house they keep loosing-off at. Go there, if you like: there's no harm in an occasional bod being seen approaching Bois Mesnil. Gerry can blow it to hell as far as we are concerned. Actually if you use your loaf, you can get from there to our o.p. under cover. *Under cover, if you please!* Visitors to o.p.'s seldom give pleasure to the occupants, so don't go taking a bloody great staff-car out there, will you? In fact we suggest that you move from div as far as this la Languette ridge on a motor bike with the armoured brigade before dawn. All lights *verboten*, of course. The elephants swing about a bit, so a bike will be handy if you are forced into the ditches. Do the rest on your flat feet. O.K.? Oh, when you get there, our man's name is Pringle.'

* * *

Tanks were medieval, thought Jack Sherard, both when they lurched through narrow medieval streets or when they raced with whirling penants of dust across the plains. He had once shared a route with an armoured brigade and had no wish to do so again, even by daylight; so he arranged with movement control to go a different way next morning.

An open main road, which would certainly be under enemy observation, ran along the crest of the forward slope he had to reach. He approached this road on foot making towards a clump of trees a quarter of a mile to his right, where he could cross without appearing on a sky line.

The road was quite empty: it seemed that no one would ever come this way again; and no bird sang. The silence was unnerving. But on the other side he could drop into cover and find his way to Bois Mesnil. Indeed he could already see down there one of its pepper-pot turrets bosomed high in splintered trees. He crossed over in the continuing hush.

During the next quarter of an hour nothing much seemed to be happening; but mortaring started just as he reached the Bois Mesnil lane. And as soon as he sought shelter in an empty stable, a near-miss brought down a fresh trickle of rubble through a hole in its roof.

21

During this unpleasantness he looked at the back of the big house across the yard. Many of its shutters were either hanging or had fallen from their hinges. During a lull he walked over and got in through a smashed door. The kitchen must have been abandoned in haste: iron pans with long handles hung from the walls; and among the recent debris of plaster on the table were a battery of knives and a vegetable chopper.

The ceiling was also down in the salon. In the library adjoining, books were scattered everywhere; and he picked up a *Decameron* with engravings by Gravelot. He found an Eisen La Fontaine; and he did not notice that by the time he had put what lay around him in some sort of order, the mortaring had stopped. He was examining a binding when he was startled by an appalling twang from the next room. This was followed by frantic jangling. He dropped on one knee and peered round the door.

In the wreckage of the salon a goat was struggling to disentangle itself from the innards of an overturned pianoforte. He caught sight of himself reflected in a pier-glass: he had become entirely grey (white almost); eyebrows, face and battledress were powdered with dust. He remained quite still as the goat freed itself and made off. It was then that he noticed a painting partly jammed behind a table: it had fallen across the lower part of the pier-glass and split the corner of its own frame.

When he had recovered himself he worked the picture loose and propped it against a wall. It was an oil painting on a good quality double-primed canvas. It showed a summer garden with figures seen from within a room that had open french windows. The time of day represented was that magical moment of first dusk when colour glows and quivers, seeming to transcend the confines of form. Cast shadows on grass and bare earth were interwreathed skeins, thinly painted—perhaps rubbed-in with a brush stub. These marks were of teasing tonal complexity and colour, clashing deliciously with what could be seen of the room's interior. The room, indeed, still shared the daylight glow. But the as yet scarcely identifiable warmth of a shaded lamp had begun to spread a yellowness over near-by lace curtains, patterned wall paper and white damask table cloth. It was, however, a scene with figures. Three ladies in white hats and long cotton dresses were about to enter from the garden.

'My God!' said Jack Sherard. 'It must be a Bonnard or a Vuillard!'

*   *   *

On the evening of the day that Jack Sherard had recognised that same Vuillard in the Reverend Martin Chew's attic, he travelled to London by train with Mrs Capper. The next day he called by appointment on Rowland Mallender at the Cornford Gallery in Duke Street.

As he arrived, he saw Rowland's secretary step into the street to look at the colour of some nylons she had bought during the lunch hour.

'Oh, Mr Sherard,' she said prettily, 'Mr Mallender won't be a moment. Actually he's just selling a Renoir.'

'Crikey! What, all of it?'

'Quite a big share, I think,' she said, but still turning her purchase this way and that. Although the gallery blazed with light for the sale of Renoirs, *she* used the light of day for anything that really mattered to her . . .

'Look all right?' he asked, winking. She blushed. 'I'll wait inside, if I may,' he suggested, 'and inspect your nice lithographs.'

Master Rowley, as he was known to most people in the business, was certainly the man to handle any Vuillard newly come upon the town. His own origins were mysterious:

he himself had come upon the London scene about twenty years since with some paintings by Bonnard that he had been in no hurry to sell. Their value had risen; and with these under his arm, as it were, he had joined the respectable —if no longer actively prosperous—Cornford Gallery. His position there had been strengthened by the spectacular success of the Bonnard Winter Exhibition at Burlington House in 1966. By now Master Rowley *was* the Cornford, even if he himself did not quite match its former image. Eyebrows—and prices—were apt to be raised at this end of Duke Street.

'Well, Jack, my boy,' said Master Rowley, with rosy dewlaps quivering, 'from what you say,' and he rubbed his hands, 'I should guess that you have got hold of one of the Nabis.* And what could be nicer? Signed or unsigned, what's that among friends? If you think it's a Vuillard, it probably *is*. You can give it a history, I hope? You say it's temporarily in someone else's house? And where might the owner be, if you don't mind me asking?'

'No one knows. I have been round his old haunts in London. There's no news of him.'

'Um! Like the loitering heirs of city directors, he has vamoosed and left no addresses. He's no forger, I hope?'

'If he were, I am sure you could detect his forgeries.'

'We have our methods, Jack.'

'No doubt. Look, Rowley. I first saw this picture years ago during the war. I was alone under bombardment in a blitzed house in Normandy, and the nearest officer on duty was in an observation post round the corner. I told him this picture should not be left there and I also passed the information to a man in Civil Affairs at Headquarters. I never did find out what happened to it because all hell broke loose next day and everyone was up and off.'

*Group name given to Bonnard and his associates.

'My dear Jack, you must have been a terrifyingly martial figure, brandishing your claymore, or whatever! So you think your fellow crept out of his hidey-hole to liberate that Vuillard before he began his gallop to Berlin?'

'Yes. He probably took it off its stretcher and rolled it inside an empty shell case. Very sensibly.'

'You haven't told me who the original and lawful owner may be.'

'No.'

'Have you any idea, Jack?'

'None.'

'You don't say, either, where the picture is now.'

'No, I don't. It's not in my charge, you see.'

'Pity, say I.'

'That's as may be, Rowley.'

Master Rowley rocked back in his chair with crossed hands clasping an ankle: the soles of his shoes were small and thin. 'Look, Jack,' he said, 'Vuillard often painted to commission. This was probably a group family-portrait which never went through a dealer's hands before reaching that house in Normandy. We could now find out who lived there. As you and I very well know, the picture would be all the better for a well-established provenance. But such enquiries, however discreet, might embarrass the brutal and licentious soldiery involved.'

'If any.'

'As you say, if any.'

'It might even cause a stink in a remote English village, Jack.'

'I don't think I know what you are talking about, Rowley.'

'Do you not, Jack? Of course, the hopeful peddler of a slightly soiled Vuillard may have done a bunk, eh? Have you got all your own pictures ready for the show at the Whitechapel?'

25

'Since we are changing the subject, yes, thank you.'

'Only sort of changing it, Jack. I *am* looking forward to your show. *And* to the boiled beef sandwiches at that exotic place next door. Not that beef alone would lure me to Aldgate East. It should be a prestigious turning-point in your career, my boy. A pity you had to leave your beautiful Hammersmith studio just now. You moved to a dire country-side, hear tell.'

'I don't know what you heard, Rowley.'

'All those duck down there madly winging their way over level wastes into the sunset. Or sunrise, I suppose, on that coast? After all, you are not getting ready for a sporting show at the Tryon Gallery. No need of punt guns, decoys and the snares of the fowler just to track down a Vuillard.'

'As you say, Rowley, I am a city slicker, like you. But the offer of accommodation was convenient.'

'Very, very convenient, I should say, as things turned out. But if you'll excuse me I must get this nice Renoir taken round the corner before some soldier-man pops it in a shell case. The very idea! What people will do for money! You'll let me know, won't you, what you want done about that thing, um? Anything legal, that is.'

III

FRANK FENWICK could smell sea air. He was on his way by motor car to pick up at Saint Osyth the Reverend Martin Chew, vicar of Saint Osyth and Saint Sebastian Sibling. He also hoped to be met there by an elderly architect, Mr Gregory Poleyn, lately of the firm of Poleyn and Schynbald.

The three of them (himself, as Rural Dean, the incumbent and the architect) intended, under the Redundant Churches Measure 1968, to examine whatever fabric might remain of Saint Sebastian's ancient eyot church. Church and churchyard were closed. The live inhabitants of this diminishing community had long since moved inland towards Saint Osyth Sibling.

His road ran beside the high embankment of the Thumbelow Drain. On the other side birds flew up and resettled in the barley fields as he drove past. A thundering noise behind caused him to hug the verge. An empty truck, closely followed by another sped past on the way to near-by gravel workings. The backs of both vehicles bounced noisily over pot holes. Saint Osyth ahead was marked by a smudge of trees round the vicarage. Larks hitherto had been well-content with the lonely spot. What of Mrs Chew?

The parsonage house at Saint Osyth was tall and narrow, with turrets and gables. Plate glass in the windows blackly reflected surrounding trees. It was the sort of house that in a sleazy London suburb would have been taken over by an insurance agency. His heart sank as he drove between the

Wellingtonias at the vicarage gates; but at that moment the front door—painted red, he noted—swung open and the vicar gaily hastened down the steps with an armful of documents and with a shaggy dog slithering at his heels.

'Morning, Canon! Down, Tarquin! Down, sir! Heel!' he shouted cheerfully; and he dumped his papers on Mr Fenwick's motor car bonnet, at the same time leaving a faintly perceptible spray of spit on the windscreen.

'Good morning, Chew,' said Mr Fenwick as he opened the passenger door. 'Do get in.'

Mr Chew did so: plans and papers cascaded among the gear levers as, in a sort of game of musical chairs, he repelled Tarquin from boarding by giving him a sturdy hand-off. He groped under his feet. 'Poor sort of morning, um?' he said. 'Oh, by the way, Poleyn sends his apologies. He's in bed with lumbago. But he sent some papers if I can find them all. I expect he thinks they may help, um?'

Mr Fenwick was reminded of some fictional cleric. Could it be Mr Collins? Surely not. Could it be Mr Elton? Chew would be more good-natured. No matter. An unrolled plan slithered to his feet and re-coiled itself. More papers fell into his lap; a copy of a report that Mr Poleyn's firm had produced on the church, well before the 1955 Act of Parliament required regular inspections to be made.

Mr Fenwick became more cheerful. 'This is excellent Chew. Most kind of him. I see this was done in 1924, eh? That would be before either of us was in the diocese. It would have been made for old Canon Template. He must have been an unusually fabric-conscientious incumbent for those days. More honour to him! Have you looked at any of this?'

'Well, no. I . . . '

'You have scarcely had time, I imagine. But I think that if I look at it very quickly before we start, it may save us quite a lot of time at the other end. As I remember, what is now the belfry at Saint Sebastian is the original wood structure from which the rest grew. Um, "plastered rubble construction with some limestone, brick and timber . . . timber belfry . . . " um, "brick chancel of two bays dating from the late eighteenth century . . . sash windows north and south . . . no east window . . . pine wainscot . . . Holy table of sixteenth century now set without footpace against east wall." Um! "Riddel posts but no curtains or dorsal . . . " oh, "centred below wall plate are three cherubs in Coade Stone . . . "'

'Whatever's "Coade Stone", canon?'

'It's an artificial cast stone, a late eighteenth-century patent. The figure of Britannia on the pediment of Stourminster Shire Hall is in Coade Stone. There's lots of it about.'

He read in silence with greater concentration, 'Below the cherubs hangs a most strange, richly-framed picture of Our Lady. I strongly advise that expert opinion be sought on this . . . ' He folded the papers. 'Well, Chew,' he said, 'it seems that in 1924, when this was written, a painting hung in the sanctuary. Is it there, now?'

'Um, well . . . '

'My information is that the altar table was taken to the new church at Pentlesham-juxta-Mare.'

Chew brightened. 'That's correct. By Faculty. Before my time. But just after I came here Canon Martin borrowed the communion rail.'

'"*Borrowed*" a communion rail . . . ?'

'Well, he *took* it! I helped him with it into the back of his van. It was for some church he was interested in at Carless End.'

'Were there any other furnishings, ornaments, fittings, pictures?' He broke off realising an ascending scale in his voice. He was becoming impatient. But Mr Chew said, cheerfully enough, 'There must have been something, eh?

Pews, for example. I seem to remember they were big, like open railway trucks. But as to carvings or pictures, I shouldn't think so. Not anything valuable, that is. Eh?'

'Well, we had better find out when we get there. We keep on past the Hurdlemakers and the old school at Saint Sebastian and then bear right, under the Drain, don't we? Have you come across Mr Sherard yet at the school? And what has happened to the strange Mr Pringle?'

*   *   *

The Hurdlemakers at Saint Sebastian was said to serve the worst beer in all the Siblings—some called it sheep dip, others dillwater. The hamlet, as they passed the Green, did indeed seem a rural slum. Mr Chew said that it was a pity the school had had to be closed. Mr Fenwick suggested that the brewers might have been glad of an excuse to close the pub.

'There's that artist's van outside the school,' said Mr Chew. 'But I don't think he's working there today since there is no sign of his little Austin runabout. You see, he doesn't live here. He stays at a hotel in Stourminster, it seems. Who's this Mrs Capper, then?'

'Oh, so you've met her, Chew? She's Margaret Capper, the actress.'

'Oh, *that* Margaret Capper. Quite well known, eh? Why should she be seen in my parish, do you suppose?'

'My wife tells me that she's now doing a London season of Elizabethan tragedies. If you saw her here she was probably looking at Mr Sherard's new work. They are very old friends . . . '

The road left the Green went under a bridge and passed the village shop-cum-post office.

'A bit of a struggle to keep a shop going here, wouldn't you say, Chew?'

'Certainly, canon. It's run by a man called Plumb. His sister, a Mrs Neame and her husband run the Hurdlemakers. They say that Plumb and his sister, Clara Neame, run the village.'

'We must be getting near your church, or what's left of it. Does anyone use this road, apart from the people living at that biggish house?'

'Very well-off people,' said Mr Chew with something of a glow. 'He's a printer somewhere: the name is Bestworth.'

'Helpful?'

'I hardly ever see them. They are summer visitors, who bought the place about five years ago. They keep a five-ton sloop at Renters Hard: they lay it up here during the winter. They are not church people.'

'Nor were the previous owners, I am told. It's an odd place for anyone to have chosen to build a house this size. I must ask Poleyn about it.'

The road followed the course of a brook or 'shot'. This was hidden from them by overgrown thorn and elder. But the other verge was open to meadows, mazy with runnels and pricked out with pollarded willows. A herd of Friesian cattle mooched darkly along the low skyline. The only house now in sight was the 'biggish' one they had just mentioned. It was called Parflete. Its smooth red brick and clipped macrocarpa hedges looked well cared for.

'Do they employ anyone in the village?'

'A gardener, I believe. When they first came a Mrs Tyler use to "do for them" as a daily. She's an, er, rather unsatisfactory sort of woman, um?'

They slowed down. A name-board hung from wrought-iron trivets set in the mown verge. There was a drive-in to a garage which was standing open and empty. Next to it, also unoccupied, was a larger structure with open sides and a shingle roof. The sides were draped with sheets of polythene which filled and rustled in the light breeze—an irritating melancholy sound. Mr Chew explained that this was where the Bestworths laid up their boat in the winter. 'They'll be away now, no doubt, if it's good sailing weather. It certainly looks as if no one were at home.'

There was a gap opposite in the overgrown hedge beyond which, on the farther side of the brook, they could now see a small church with a weather-boarded belfry. The church-yard looked desolate, the church less so.

'Well, Chew,' said Frank Fenwick, 'I don't suppose we shall find any one in your church, either.'

* * *

The church had been built in the fourteenth century on an island among freshets making for the tide water. It could now be reached on foot by a plank bridge (or 'overshot') and by a ford made for the carriage-folk. The ford had also been provided with stepping stones for the man propelling the Siblings hand-bier. Frank Fenwick reckoned that these same stones would disembowel the under parts of his motor car. He therefore backed off the road into the empty boat-house at Parflete. The two clergymen crossed to the church by footbridge.

The churchyard was quite overgrown with grass and bramble, but there were some recent beaten-down tracks between the headstones. They followed these to a door on the far side of the church; but they found the porch sadly fallen-in. There was a dead fox under the wreckage; and hanging laths threatened a further collapse of tiles and plaster if they tried to reach the door.

'Most un-*four*-chinit!' said Mr Chew, swinging his heavy key. 'Shall we try further along?'

'Further along' there was, indeed, a smaller, 'priest's' entrance to the chancel. But they found that this door had already been forced, and quite recently, to judge from the raw look of the splintered wood.

'I don't know whether this is unfortunate or not,' said Mr Fenwick, 'but at least I think we can get in.' He squeezed through, but turned back to say, 'There's a most unpleasant smell, Chew. Another dead fox, do you suppose? Phew! It's disgusting! All the same, we had better have a look round if you can bear it.'

The chancel, within, looked very desolate. High on the wall at the east end, and looking in need of a good wash behind the ears, were the Coade Stone cherubs. A broken rush-seated chair stood against the wainscot where the altar table should have been. There was certainly no picture above it: only, on varnished panels, the Ten Commandments painted in *art nouveau* script.

The floor was tiled and very dusty. It was littered with crumbs of plaster and there were confused marks where one or more persons had trampled: one set of footprints was certainly larger than the other. Mr Fenwick stood well back, avoiding these tracks. His eye was caught by a little red paper disc such as may be stuck to documents in 'place of a seal'.

He turned, 'I can't stand this stink, Chew! Before we can do anything else we had better find out what's causing it. I should think it's down there among those pews in the nave.'

It wasn't another dead fox. It was a very dead Thomas Pringle.

IV

'THE REVEREND has found us another body, Charles,' said Detective Chief Superintendent Quill into his office telephone.

'Good Lord, sir!' answered Detective Inspector Glover. 'Not again? And which Reverend? I take it you mean Canon Fenwick out at Fleury Feverel?'

'None other, Charles. But not in his own parish this time. The cadaver is at Saint Sebastian Sibling.' He gave the map reference. 'And don't ask me what the good canon was doing out there. He was with the vicar; so I am sure ecclesiastical protocol was being observed. But, my goodness, how glad the Press will be to learn of another church murder! No, it wasn't in a burial vault this time.* It has apparently been battered with a cast-iron grating and shoved under a pew.'

'Do we know who it is, sir?'

'Not yet. The local vicar, who telephoned from the village post office, says that from what he could see of the shoes and trousers it may be a Mr Thomas Pringle who's gone missing from the parish recently. Bit of a mystery chap, it seems. I got on to Best at Division and he is sending someone to hold the fort until we arrive. Can you get out there with the usual outfit? The parsons got into the church, they say, through a door that had already been broken open in the chancel. They seem to have kept their heads. The floor was very dusty, with a lot of confused footprints up the top end where the

* Worse Than Death.

altar would have been; and we are told to look out for a
little red paper seal which may have come off a legal document—lawyer, do you suppose, nosing about? The body,
they say, is back in the main part of the church. Nave, isn't
it? It is fully clothed but fairly far gone. We may have difficulty in moving it in one piece. Nasty! It is held under the
seat by a grating taken from the duct for the old heating
pipes. And from the mess on this grating they think, as Fleet
Street says, "foul play cannot be ruled out".'

'Did the parsons move anything, sir?'

'They say, not. Except to open the door of the pew. The
pews are big ones, it seems, like loose boxes. They say that we
will have no trouble in spotting their own tracks in the dust.
They deliberately kept away from any others when they
realised that the church had already been broken into. I must
be with the Chief Constable in ten minutes; so I'll join you
at Saint Seb later. If the body does turn out to be Thomas
Pringle's, he lived at the old school opposite the Hurdlemakers on the Green. His cousin, a Mr Sherard, seems to
have been there recently. Interest him in our plight, Charles,
that is if you can find him. And take a look at the size of his
boots. Oh, and the school premises might be made available
to us as our incident office. See you soon, Charles. Good
hunting!'

*   *   *

When Chief Superintendent Quill reached Saint Sebastian
Sibling he was pleased to find police vehicles standing outside the old school buildings. When he entered he found that
Detective Sergeant Simmons was already organising an
office.

'Sir,' said the Sergeant, introducing a tall thin stranger,
'This is Mr Sherard, an artist who has been working here
for the last few weeks. He comes from 5 Sandby Studios,

35

Hammersmith. He has said that he would be glad of a word with you. I have fitted up an office in the adjoining house for you and Inspector Glover. The Inspector is still down at the scene of the incident, sir.'

'Thank you, Sergeant. Mr Sherard, perhaps you will kindly join us in the other room? My name is Quill, and I am the Detective Chief Superintendent of the County Police at Stourminster.'

Mr Sherard bowed.

'The gentleman was on the point of returning to London, when we arrived, sir,' said the Sergeant as they moved into the front room of the school-house. 'He had just finished loading his van. When we told him, sir, that a body had been found down at the church, which might be that of his missing cousin, he was able to make that identification.'

'It must have been an unpleasant duty, Mr Sherard.'

'It was quite horrible.'

'Allow me to express our condolences, sir.'

'Thank you. But he and I saw very little of each other; and I don't know what I can tell you.' He sat on the chair that the Sergeant brought forward. The Chief Superintendent noted that the neatly-shod feet were distinctly long and narrow.

'Your, er, Inspector, is it?' said Mr Sherard, 'asked me to wait for you here before I made any, er, "statement", as he called it.'

'It would certainly help us if you could answer a few questions, Mr Sherard.'

'Yes?'

'When did you come to Saint Sebastian?'

'On the twelfth of August—that's three weeks ago, isn't it? I have been staying at a pub in Stourminster and have used this place purely as somewhere to finish my paintings.'

'Finish?'

36

'I had to leave my London studio. The scheme or notation for the pictures was already settled by then.'

'Not local colour, sir,' said the Sergeant. Quill noticed Mr Sherard's nose twitching. Perhaps the Sergeant noticed this too. He hastened to alter the term, 'The gentleman explained that he had not been out sketching round here, sir.'

'You were packing up today?' asked Quill.

'I can stay on at Stourminster for a day or two if . . . '

'Well, sir, thank you: that would be more convenient for us. You will be needed for the inquest, if you please . . . evidence of identification, and so on . . . '

Jack Sherard was looking at his van through the window. 'All right, but I must get my stuff up to London today. The gallery is near Aldgate East Station.'

'Whitechapel High Street, eh? Shall you be wanting to stay and arrange your pictures when you get there?'

'Oh, no. Not yet, Mr Quill. The Gallery Director will do the hanging in about ten days' time. I must be there when he starts, if you please.'

'In that case, sir, if the pictures are expected today I could arrange for one of our drivers to take them for you.'

There was a short silence. Then Jack Sherard said, 'How very kind of you, Chief Superintendent; but I should like to see everything safely handed over. Perhaps, if it is not asking too much, if I went with your driver he could then bring me back to Stourminster?'

'Bring you back gladly. And I'll notify Division up there so that there'll be no trouble while your van is being unloaded.'

He then proceeded to more personal questions: full name, age, regular domicile, and so on. 'May I take it that you and the late Mr Thomas Pringle were first cousins on your mother's side of the family?'

'Yes.'

'And his age, please, when he died?'

'About fifty-five. His father married my aunt in 1915: one of the "khaki" weddings, no doubt. Until his grandfather died my cousin actually went to this village school. Then he went to the Grammar School at Stourport: he would have been ten or eleven years old then.'

'Was his father—your uncle—the Mr Reginald Pringle who used to be an estate-agent at Stourport?'

'Yes. My uncle took up that occupation in 1919 after he had been demobilised. He moved from here to Stourport at that time.'

'"From here"? The school-house?'

'Ah, no. I beg your pardon. From Saint Sebastian. You see, they had all been living with my late cousin's grandfather in that biggish house which the old gentleman had built down by the church. I've no idea whose it is now.'

'It *is* a biggish house. If I may say so, it must have been unusual for a child from such a place to have been sent to the village school? Were they not fairly rich?'

'Undoubtedly. The grandfather certainly was. But he was a socialist of sorts. As soon as he died the younger family moved to Stourport. They may have been pleased to leave and get their child to another school. My cousin never explained to me why he chose to return to Saint Sebastian. The school-house may have been one of his father's property investments. Easier to occupy, perhaps, than let or sell.'

'Was Thomas Pringle in business as an estate agent with his father at Stourport?'

'No. He had been until 1939 when he went into the army. (He was a territorial gunner.) After the war he joined another firm in Hammersmith. He may have thought that Stourport would be a bit tame.'

'Used you to see him in London, Mr Sherard?'

'Oh, I sometimes *saw* him, since his offices were near my

studio. But our occupations and interests had become so very different, you will understand, that I was surprised to find when I needed a studio, that he knew so much of what I was doing. He actually came to see me about it.'

'You didn't consult him?'

'Certainly not. He literally came to see me with a surprise offer to lend me this extraordinary building on the edge of the Stour Siblings. And that was the last time that I saw him alive . . . '

'Oh? You fixed it up there and then that you should move in here? Time of arrival and all?'

'Yes. I was to drive down with all my gear. I even wrote to him confirming everything. So that, since no one was here to let me in I reckon I was damned lucky to have found the key.'

'Can you give us his former London address?'

He gave a number in the King's Road. 'It's somewhere near the World's End. He was in digs with a Mrs Prosit. I saw her when I was last in London and she said that he was to come back to her for the whole of this month. Moving out of here for me, you see. Only he never turned up or let her know.'

'When was it that you saw *her*?'

'On the twenty-fifth—Wednesday, last week. I went up late on Tuesday and stayed the night with one of my friends and returned to Stourminster the following evening.'

'Your friend's name and address, if you please?'

There was a pause, and he looked up sharply. 'Goodness, Chief Superintendent! It was a Mrs Capper.' He gave an address in Notting Hill. 'And let me say, since I see that you will want to know: next morning I started to ask round for news of my cousin; I wanted to hand this place back to him. I called first at the office where he used to work and then on Mrs Prosit.' He gave both addresses. 'After lunch I had to do some business with a Mr Rowland Mallender of the Cornford Gallery in Duke Street.'

'Picture business?'

'Yes. Then I took a train from Liverpool Street and returned to Stourminster.'

'That has been very helpful. You wanted to hand over these premises to your cousin and went up to London to see if you could discover what had happened to him. No one you spoke to could tell you anything about his movements?'

'That is correct.'

'Can you think of any one else who might be able to do so?'

'No one. There *might* be someone hereabouts. But *I* wouldn't know.'

'Quite so, sir. And you say that all the time you have been here since the twelfth you haven't had a walk round the village. You have just driven backwards and forwards between here and the Crown and Cresset?'

'That is correct, except for this morning.'

'Ah! This morning you kindly went with Inspector Glover to the churchyard, wasn't it?'

He grimaced. 'Yes, my cousin's body was on a stretcher outside the church. I was able to identify it.'

'And you have never been there before, or inside the church at Saint Sebastian Sibling?'

'Good gracious, yes! I have not only set foot in its holy places. I have even wriggled along a channel under the floor. Builders call it a crawlway or creep trench. You know, covered with an iron grating.'

V

ALTHOUGH THE 1914 WAR (from which his father would never return) was now over, seven-year-old Jack Sherard was still on the look-out for Zeppelins during the train journey to Stourminster with his mother's maid, a pleasant girl called Mabel.

'For land's sake, Master Jack,' she said, 'you won't never see none o' them no more! They's only about in war times, same's I said. Us shot 'em all down. Bang! Bang! Woosh! See that great big church over there? That'll be Sturmster. Mrs Pringle do be waiting fer us arter this long ole journey. Lawks! Come on train! Do us'll be late fer our tea . . . '

The train which had been creaking to the top of a gradient now obligingly went into a bump and clatter. The hanging-down sleeve of a raincoat on the luggage rack started to swing; and Master Jack, who had stood up to look for the promised land, was neatly shot back into his seat. He looked round shyly to see if he had been made a fool of.

'Shall we pass through Cuffley, Mabel?' he asked.

'Cuffley? Get along with you! Whatever next?' she said, glancing at the other travellers. And she, to his embarrass-ment, explained that Cuffley was where she had seen a Zeppelin shot down. The little boy, she said, thought that he was being taken there to see another.

Dismayed at this betrayal, he stretched out his legs and looked at his boots.

The purpose of the journey with Mabel had *not* been

explained to his satisfaction. Nor had much else of late. He thought of 'Now' as a dark tunnel with no view at either end. He scarcely remembered his father, who had not come back from the war; although that was to have been the arrangement. And something now seemed to be happening in Ireland to his mother's father, whom he knew much better. His mother had gone there, leaving her son to be taken by Mabel to stay with his aunt Florence at the 'curious' house near Stourminster.

He had not been told what was 'curious' about it. Nor had he liked to ask since, when he had overheard the remark, he had been a little pitcher with long ears. He did not see what could be curious about his own mother's sister, and could only hope that things would be all right.

He raised his eyes from his boots to the distant sky line. Birds were flying round the great tower of Stourminster cathedral. The train rumbled between the girders of a bridge; and as these flicked by he saw that he was being carried over a wide sheet of water. He got up and pressed his face to the window of the carriage: there were islands of reeds and a great flotilla of swans. 'Tide's making,' said someone.

The train went on slowly through the outskirts of a town.

'Is this Stourminster?' he asked, excited.

'No need to get out afore we're there, love. Hold up then!' The train had once more suddenly stopped and Mabel held him by the back of his jersey. He knew that she would say, 'Ups a daisy!'

They waited. The train hissed. A road bridge had appeared, running beside the railway. Men were ranged along its far parapet watching a game of cricket. He jumped up excitedly, again. Stands and marquees could be seen below. Cricket! He had an idea that this visit to his aunt was going to be all right.

*　　*　　*

It *had* been all right so far. Darkness had fallen by the time he had had supper in the kitchen, been given a bath and put to bed by Mabel in a room 'under the roof', as she said.

In the morning he could see what she meant by this: the ceiling sloped so that it was like being in a tent. The window was at the end of a little tunnel. To see out of it he had to kneel on a padded seat.

He looked straight into the sun. When he shaded his eyes he could see water and islands everywhere, and, away in the distance, shipping. There was the sound of crying gulls, and when he leaned out of the window he could hear small birds rustling and hopping behind his head. He was startled by the clap of a pigeon's wings as it shot up from the leads on which it had been strutting.

'Where's my boy this lovely morning?' asked Mabel from within the room. 'You'll be having your breakfast in the kitchen with your cousin Tom as soon as you're washed and dressed. Then, if you're good, Mrs Pringle is going to take you both to see the master in his bird room.'

'What's a "bird room", Mabel?'

'Gracious! How should I know? You'll have to wait and see, won't you, love? It'll be full of birds, I shouldn't wonder. Mrs Gardner, and she's the cook, says the master spends the morning up there, without fail. She says it's all he lives for.'

'"All he lives for"?' he cried, appalled.

'It's time you was in that bathroom, young man! *And* washed and dressed! *And* not asking me so many questions! "Curious" indeed! Curiosity, I'm told, killed the cat. Perhaps there may be a letter from Ireland for a certain person, if the post comes.'

'Oh, Mabel, will there?'

'I said, "perhaps", love. All depends on the cat's tail.'

'"Cat's tail"?'

'Irish Mail. Come, get along, do!'

There *was* a letter for him from his mother downstairs. So *that* was all right.

*　　*　　*

The 'master' was not his uncle, Reginald Pringle, but his uncle's father. It seemed a long way to the master's bird room. His aunt did not take him up but left him in charge of his cousin. The treads of the stair were wide and the risers shallow. The stair carpet was thick, rough, and of a plain oatmeal colour, not the Turkey pattern to which he was used at home. Moreover the inside woodwork of this house was unpainted, and, even more unusual, the walls were of unplastered brick.

The bird room, when they got there, seemed to be all windows with book shelves under them. Here, every day, Mr Mostyn Pringle sat on a swivel chair beside a telescope. On each window-ledge field-glasses were to hand.

Mr Pringle had a small tuft of white beard, and his adam's apple could be seen above a loose-fitting grey flannel shirt collar and knitted tie. He wore a pepper-and-salt Norfolk jacket, knickerbockers, black stockings and black boots. He did not look at the boys when they came in.

Jack's cousin silently tiptoed to one of the windows and stared, or pretended to stare, out of it; while Jack waited to be spoken to. Before long the old gentleman did begin to ask him a few questions. Then he told him that he would *not* be taken to a church service while he was at Saint Sebastian Sibling; but he advised him to 'visit the edifice, because it is a fine and plain one', and to 'play with Thomas, your little cousin, anywhere round about, if you do not disturb my birds or fall into water . . . ' 'With birds and water', he added, 'we are liberally provided. But with other little boys and girls we are less well-stocked. Play with any of the village boys unless they want to go bird-nesting.'

He was not encouraged at home to talk to 'other' children unless these had been 'looked at'. He well knew what this meant. He even wondered whether his mother had 'looked at' his cousin Tom—'Thomas'. Tom seemed sly and spoke with a whining sing-song. When Tom showed him the garden they were at once joined by another boy who certainly would not have stood being looked at. He was snotty-nosed with a hanging-open mouth and a hoarse voice. Jack could scarcely understand a word he said, although, in fact he spoke only to Tom, who was obviously frightened of him. When they moved out of the garden into the road, Jack did not know what to do; but since he had been told to play with the village boys, he decided to follow. He was then at once adopted by a rough-haired terrier, who seemed to know that entry to the garden was not for him but that any person issuing from it would be fair company. When the other two set forward the dog looked to see that Jack followed.

They crossed the runnel to the churchyard, hopping from stone to stone, well splashed by the dog's frolic bounds. As they waited in the long grass on the other side Tom became increasingly frightened; but the other boy, whose name was Johnny Plumb, took no notice until they were warned by the dog that someone else was coming. Whereupon they hid behind gravestones, and an old gentleman walked slowly round the church to open a door on the far side. This was the Reverend Julius Template, the vicar of Saint Sebastian Sibling; and he was arriving, as was his daily wont, to recite the Divine Office. A few minutes later he signified his intention to perform this God-ward act by ringing a bell. The dog, an accustomed spectator, duly thumped his tail.

Jack, not knowing why they should have had to hide, now supposed that they could go home or move elsewhere, bird-nesting only excepted. But Tom was beginning to snivel as his uncouth abettor pointed to some unused heating pipes

45

piled against the west wall of the church. Here a dark cavity at ground level had been opened for connection with a boiler-house. Tom Pringle was pushed into this hole by Johnny Plumb, who indicated that Jack should follow. The whimpering dog was left to guard their rear.

They began to crawl darkly forward; but when it became lighter, Jack realised that they were in a trench covered by an iron grille. The sound they made seemed very loud, and Johnny soon signalled for them to move more slowly. When they rose to their knees and could press their faces against the under-side of the grating, he could see, on his left, sheer panelling and to the right the upper part of some pews with doors. One of these was open. Johnny nudged and they slowly raised the grating so that their eyes came level with the floor. As their heads continued to rise they could see the old gentleman. He was seated and words formed silently on his lips.

They then sank below floor level, carefully lowering the grille into its socket. Since they could not turn, they had to crawl backwards to the outer air. This seemed the longer and more difficult part of the ordeal; but they eventually emerged, hot and filthy, to find the dog waiting.

Was it all over? Jack had not enjoyed this pointless adventure. Tom had promptly burst into tears. But Johnny rolled his lubber length about in the grass, roaring with laughter. Then he set off towards the road and cleared the water splash with a wild leap. The dog had followed more circumspectly.

VI

OLD-MAN'S-BEARD tapped faintly against a window in the dusty church; but the sound sharpened as a scatter of rain hit the glass. The Chief Superintendent had joined Inspector Glover, officer in charge at the scene of the crime. The Divisional Surgeon had made a preliminary examination and the body had been removed. Photographs had been taken and sundry chalk-marks were in evidence at the opening to the pew by which they stood. Beside it a length of grating had been removed from over the heating duct.

'Back of the head bashed in about three weeks ago, eh, Charles? I agree with you that there were two persons here at the material time. Pringle and another seem to have been moving about in the dust at the top end. The other had smaller feet than poor wretched Pringle. Any finger prints?'

'We got some up at the top end, there. Someone, deceased as it turns out, had been folding back the varnished panels of those Ten Commandments.'

'Thou shalt not touch.'

'Certainly not: but Pringle did.'

'Why should the late Thomas Pringle stand on the seat of a chair to finger the tables of the law? I see that they are on four panels. I presume that they fold back from the centre. Is or was there anything behind?'

'Plastered wall, dust and cobwebs. There are marks where

some rectangular object had been fixed. There's a cill that has been hastily dusted; and someone seems to have steadied himself against the back wall. There's a dirty mark of a gloved hand—smallish, with a hole over the tip of the index finger and a slit down the side of the thumb. Cotton gloves, probably. Too small for deceased. So, as you said, sir, there were two of them moving about up there. I would suggest that the search for whatever they were after continued near this pew. The grating had been taken up. Pringle was probably bending to look into the trench when, woosh! He was bashed on the back of the head!'

'Could the propped-up grating have fallen on him?'

'Unlikely, sir. Or if it did, it would not by itself have had the weight to crush his skull. I should say that A. N. Other had hold of it when he suddenly took a swing. To do so he may even have been standing on the seat of the pew.'

The Chief Superintendent raised an eyebrow.

'Well, sir, shall we say that it seems most likely that the blow was struck in this pew and the body bundled under a seat? And whoever the assailant may have been, it is likely that he would have been smallish. Is this Mr Sherard a small man, sir?'

'By no means, Charles. I can't show you his feet or finger-prints at the moment. He and his pictures have just gone off to Whitechapel . . . '

'Oh, are we keeping him under observation?'

'Yes, all laid on. He is to be met in London, helped in every way and brought back to Stourminster. He has undertaken to look in at Headquarters tomorrow morning.'

'Oh, good, sir. I haven't told you, but two letters from him were in deceased's pockets. Assignations you might call them. I have them in my case, sir.' And he produced two unfolded notes held between transparent plastic sheets marked respectively 'A' and 'B'.

48

'"A" was found folded away in Pringle's hip pocket note case; but the other one, "B", was just pushed down into an outer breast pocket behind his spectacles. There were no envelopes for post marks, but I think there can be no doubt they are both from Sherard.'

'Same handwriting, Charles, and each headed with Sherard's Hammersmith address. But different sorts of paper: the printed headings are not from the same typeface. Sherard actually told me he had written to Pringle confirming the time he would arrive here. This letter "A" must be it—he did in fact turn up midday on the twelfth.' 'A' read:

(A)   5, Sandby Studios,
                                 London, W6

Dear Tom   3 Aug 71
Shall arrive Thursday 12th at S. Seb. about
noon to 12.30. If you can let me in, it shd not
take me ¼ hr to unload my stuff & lock up. May
I then drive you to Stourminster & give you a
meal? I'm told the Crown & Cresset, but only too
willing defer yr local knowledge.
    most grateful yor kind & unexpected offr.
                                        Jack.

'Now "B", sir, written nearly a week later, seems to advance the appointment made in "A" to the evening of Tuesday, the tenth.'

'Sherard made no mention of that to me, Charles.'

'B' began without salutation,

5, Sandby Studios,
London, W6

9 Aug

Yes. Let's liberate it. Be with you tomorrow p.m. Telling you make the necessary arrangements.   *Jack*

'I agree, Charles. The cousins planned something together —perhaps even in this church—on Tuesday night. But what and why? From my 21 Army Group recollections "liberate" has undertones of complicity in loot although I am surprised at Sherard larding his style with out-of-date militarisms. I didn't find him altogether convincing, Charles. Why come to the Stour Siblings of all districts? He never intended to paint its landscape; and it seems a fantastic distance to have come otherwise. He brought all the stuff he was already at work on for his Whitechapel exhibition. And odd stuff it was too, from what I could see by peering into his van. Looked a lot of tatty *tachisme* to me, if that's the right word.'

'It's certainly a long way from Whitechapel.'

'And, Charles—a surprise! He said that he and his dead cousin, together with some third juvenile delinquent, used to crawl about when they were all kids, under the grating of this very church.'

'Good heavens! How very peculiar! Why did they do that?'

'He didn't say. It was his curtain line, Charles. Oh, and this third juvenile was one Johnny Plumb: he now keeps the village shop. Could there have been something hidden in the church to explain why Thomas Pringle, seemingly out of the blue, should lately have inveigled his prissy cousin to a rural slum? No evidence that this Plumb should be involved. But still . . . '

'How were the two cousins off for money, sir?'

'Well, we can find out, I suppose. *And* who gets Pringle's money now. Neither of them seems to have been exactly on the breadline. Sherard looked prosperous, and the late Pringle doesn't seem to have worked since his father died. There is a rumour that he was going to turn the building into a second village shop. That wouldn't please Mister Plumb the Postmaster. But we had better call on Plumb. Perhaps he could tell us about old times. I know it's beginning to rain, but do you mind if we walk? I want to get the feel of this Slough of Despond. It makes one wonder why anyone who could possibly live and work elsewhere should have gone to all this bother.'

'The car, sir?'

'Simmons can drive it back. He's a likely lad. He could take on the jobs at the London end, perhaps?'

* * *

The sorting office was in a small barn, roofed with rotten thatch. As they passed they saw a red bicycle propped against a half-open door, and a pair of well-filled blue trousers within. 'A Mrs Tyler, sir, part-time postwoman. She gets about, I'm told. Plumb's shop is up here, next to the call box.'

It began to rain harder as they slopped through puddles. A posting box was let into the wall beside the door of the shop. 'In we go,' said the Chief Superintendent.

There was a pervading stink within of household soap and paraffin. Water boots hung from the low ceiling and bulging sacks encroached on the floor space. Movement on the public side of the counter was further restricted by a large refrigerator. A bell had 'pinged' as they opened the door, but no one was in attendance.

Towers and pyramids of goods rose from the counter-top and from every other available surface. There was a glazed panel to the door behind them but the shop was very dark. The only window was at the back. It gave, so far as they were able to see through the packages, on to a rain-swept meadow. The place became darker still as this window-frame started to shake and shudder rhythmically: a cow was rubbing its flank against the outside of the glazing bars. Packs tottered on the cill . . .

'Shop!' called the Superintendent and rapped on the counter; but the outer door opened and closed at that moment as a large wet man squeezed in behind them. The darkness was now almost complete.

'Hur?' he said.

No one could turn or had room to move except for the Inspector who reached for a light switch. His elbow thereby dislodged four or five bags of self-raising flour. These almost soundlessly exploded as they hit the floor.

The three men stamped and coughed. The ceiling light-bulb diminished to a tawny glow as a blinding cloud of flour rose above heads and shoulders.

'Hur!' The newcomer jostled the two policemen and thrust violently between them. He could next be heard fighting the sash window and cursing the startled beast beyond. As the obscene storm subsided they faced an off-white world. Their rimed features twitched in efforts to shed casings of dough from wet skin and hair. The stranger, now on the other side of the counter, was very, very angry.

'My friend will pay,' said the Chief Superintendent. 'We are police officers enquiring into the death of a Mr Thomas Pringle. May I ask, sir, if you are Mr John Plumb, of this address?'

Mr Plumb, if it were he, spoke not a word. His bushy, and by now white eyebrows worked rapidly up and down—he looked a prophet new inspired.

'Did you know Mr Pringle?'

Flour and silence fell.

'Is it true that you are Mr John Plumb?'

No answer.

'Do you live here, in this house?'

'Hur.'

'And may I ask your age, Mr Plumb?'

'So it's *my* age, ef that's yore bizness, mister? I were born same year as world-war-wun. You heered on ut, likely? Nineteen-fourteen, ennit?' He sneezed violently and the policemen tried to back. 'Reverend Chew,' said Mr Plumb, 'found Pring'l this morning, then?'

'How did you know that, Mr Plumb?'

A pitying look. 'Reverend phoned from yere, see?' He indicated the telephone call box outside. There was another instrument nestling on a shelf behind him.

'Did you know Mr Pringle?'

'Heered on 'm.'

'For how long, Mr Plumb, had you "heard" of Thomas Pringle?'

'Recent, like.'

'Did you know that he was thinking of setting up another shop in this village?'

''Appen I did, then. Nowt to do wi' me, mister.'

'Who told you, Mr Plumb?'

Shrug. 'Wun o' me 'olesalers' reps says Bert Sawken, a chippy, bin arst fer a quote, see, to fit out Pring'ls as a shop, mister. Nowt to do wi' me, ennit? None aint arst *me* nothun!'

'Were you not on speaking terms yourself with the late Thomas Pringle?'

'I did'n say that, mister.'

'But is it true, Mr Plumb?'

'Mebbe.'

'Why, Mr Plumb?'

'Why, wot, mister? Wot's all they questions, then?'

'We have reason to believe, Mr Plumb, that you and Thomas Pringle knew one another here a long time ago.'

Silence.

'Did you know him before, Mr Plumb?'

Silence.

'Didn't his father live here at the house opposite the church?'

'I believe I bin tole 'bout an ole Pring'l yereabouts when I were a lil' ole boy. Likes o' me wouldna knew he at that time o' day, mister.'

'But you knew young Thomas Pringle if he went to school with you here in Saint Sebastian?'

'Look 'ee, mister. I don' zackerly know wot you bin fareing to ask, like . . . '

'The question is this, Mr Plumb: Were you, as a boy, at the village school here?'

''Appen I were.'

'Was Thomas Pringle also at that school?'

'Mebbe. Mebbe. Mebbe.'

'Thomas Pringle was a year or two younger than you. But you were both at school here together?'

Silence.

'*Did* you know Thomas Pringle as a boy?'

With the palm of his hand Plumb swept a big circle on the floury top of the counter, 'Long time fer to remember, mister.'

'Very well, Mr Plumb. A long time, yes. A lot of hot water could have passed through the new heating pipes at Saint Sebastian's church since you and he were boys together.

Oh, one other question: when did you last go down the road from this shop that leads past the church?'

There was a long pause. Mr Plumb consulted the whitened palm of his hand. 'Well, mister, I'm not much of a mucher fer walks these days, nor fer church neether. In course,' he added slowly, 'I bin . . . I sometimes takes the lil ole van wi' goods fer them Bestworths.'

'That's the house opposite the church?'

'Ur! Jes opposight!'

'And have you been down there within the last four weeks, say?'

He drew another circle with the tip of a finger, 'They's away see? Sailing, see? Arsted us to 'old back their mail, see? No goods. No deliveries, see? Not til six September, see?'

'Right, Mr Plumb. Have you been down that road or anywhere near the church during the last four weeks?'

'No I bleeding 'aven't!' said Mr Plumb with twitching eyebrows.

'And do you know of anybody, *anybody* except the late Thomas Pringle and the two clergymen who found him— can you think of anybody *else* who might have been down that way?'

'No I bloody can't!' he yelled, banging about and raising such a whirlwind of floury particles that, unable to draw back, the two policemen left him to it.

Outside it was still raining.

*   *   *

Sergeant Simmons knew that with a dead body discovered in the village, beards would wag all at the Hurdlemakers, but that for him to be seen in there again would be to waste his time. The divisional beat officer, however, had filled him in on local form. On Wednesdays, murder or no murder, the

landlord and his wife would take themselves off to Stourminster, leaving the bar, beery silences, beery flirtations and
beery confidences to the easy-going Mrs Tyler, the postwoman. It was her spare-time pleasure to help out whenever—and, it was said, however—she might be required.
Although Mrs Tyler could do nothing to improve the wallop
she served at the Hurdlemakers, she nevertheless enlivened
the company—rugged the breast that beauty cannot tame.

The children of the village also found her accommodating.
There was a sort of slype or roofed passage at the pub, which
led from the bar to the back yard. In this passage empty
bottles and crates were stacked for collection by the Stour-
head Brewery. The children found that if they brought
plausible empties from this place round to the front bar on a
Wednesday, Janice Tyler would allow money on them. As
the Psalmist almost has it, she paid them the things that she
never took; they knew her simpleness.

The beat officer engagingly suggested that if Simmons
could get into this passage and use it as a listening post, he
himself might cover the front of the house with a routine
appearance in the bar.

The Sergeant did in fact find the yard door to the window-
less passage unlocked. He entered, barking his shins more
than once as he groped towards the other door behind which
could be heard all the live murmur of a summer pub. He
was destined, however, to hear no good of himself.

'What for they send a softy like this, then? And us
butchered in our beds?'

'Not in our beds, fer land's sake!' wailed Janice Tyler.

'Proper massacre, gel. Blood all down the road! Reckon
one o' they sand lorries done it.'

'Nar! ye fule. That were in church!'

'Reckon driver were scared, then. When he seen what he
done, reckon he hid that in owd church.'

'Nar, nar, ye fule. That body bin hit wi' somep'n. Set-to, fightin'! ennit, Ben?'

'C'morn, Ben,' they said to the beat officer. 'Ef you baint supping a pint, as you bin arst more'n wunst, yew tell us who done it. Yew knows, that I'll lay. Out with it, mate!'

'Ar!' said Ben. 'Yew push these lads out sharp, Jan, do that'll be past Closing. Reckon that'd be trouble. Be seeing yew. G'nigh, all! G'nigh! G'nigh!'

Silence was followed by the sound of someone going. The door 'pinged' amid a few mild comments. 'Strewth! Mizzly ole sod! Come in yere, aint drunk noth'n! Aint tole us noth'n!'

'That don't know noth'n, pr'aps . . . '

'Know more'n he let on, that I'll lay.'

'Leastwise, reckon he know more'n that baby-face sarge from Sturmster.'

'Sarge me fanny, mate!'

'Well, luv,' said Janice Tyler. 'Look who's talking! You all back in Home Guard or summat? Us don't see all that many young uns in Seb at this time o' day! And that's a fact! Did useter wunst, don't doubt. If you arst me, mate, he's mebbe young. Anything wrong wi' that, then?'

'You sweet on him, Jan?'

'You mind yore business, Tom, and I'll mind mine, see? Aint seen the sarge but the wunst. He come in this morning to pass the time o' day, pleasant, like. Pleasant, see? None in here aint said noth'n. All setting around like lardy-cakes. All looking in the bottom o' their mugs. Tongues lost there or summat.'

'That baint the fust thing bin lost in that ole muck, Jan. Bit sharp now, folks, ennit?'

'Cor! I'll say!'

'Git along with ye, Bob. Sup that up, luv. Do you won't niver get 'nuther!'

57

There was a lull.

'That Pring'l a gen'elman o' leisure, then?'

'How long Pring'l bin yere?'

'Coupla quarters, reckon.'

'Eighteen munce.'

'Nigh on.'

'Aint niver done noth'n, eh?'

'That won't do noth'n now neether.'

'That I'll lay.'

'Aint even took his pension with'm.'

'They ses he were fareing to open 'nother shop, like.'

'That'd be two shops in Seb, then? That'd be suthick mighty strange?'

'Ar!'

There was silence. Water could be heard dripping in the bar. Then someone asked, 'Two shops? What you say 'bout that, Janice, girl?'

'Noth'n, then, Alfie.'

'On'y wondered, like. Reckon 'nother shop'd nark owd Johnny Plumb, Jan?'

'Dunno, Alfie. Yew arst 'm, mate. Some's I knows is allus creating cos there's only one.'

'Some creates cos there's only one boozer. Room fer two, Jan girl. As 'tis, us allus be supping this same owd muck. No offence, like.'

'Drink up, then. Do that'll be Time.'

'What for that artis' bloke come to Seb, Jan?'

'Wot for Bestworths come yere, then? Aint noth'n yere fer they, surelie?'

'Jan, yere, worked fer Bestworths; yew arst 'er, mate. C'morn, Jan, girl . . . '

'They come here along o' their boat, luv. They's more often on that than home.'

'Bestworths knew this Pring'l, Jan?'

58

'Don't arst me, Sid. That's two year since I bin with they.'

'Us knows that, Jan. But Pring'l seemingly been done in right opposight theirs. Reckon they'd know about it?'

'Well, Sid, they's now away in that rotten old boat, and bin gorn since th' end of July. Us stopped all letters, like, till September.'

'Pring'l bin gorn missing three weeks ennit? Since that night what you wasn't yere, Jan, ennit?'

'Don't arst me, luv! Reckon I'm kep busy now 'n then, luv!'

'Ar! Reckon now 'n then, girl. Us knows that, Jan! But that were the night what the new artis' bloke tooken over school, ennit?'

There was a chorus, 'Nar! Nar! . . . He tooken over Tharsday . . . Next morning, mate . . . New artis' bloke were lookin fer Pring'l's key to let un in . . . Come in yere midday, Tharsday . . . Pring'l were dead then, reckon . . . '

'Yew reckon this artis' done it, mate?'

'Don't arst me, lad! Don't know what he done!'

'Proper lar-de-dar feller. His cami-flarge painted van 'n all! Not army cami-flarge neether. That I do know, mate.'

There was a considerable lull in the talk. The Sergeant was able to lay down his pencil torch and stretch his fingers. The tap continued to drip in the bar. Somewhere in the wainscot he could hear mice.

Then Janice Tyler spoke again. She sounded puzzled. 'What's that you say, Sid? The cami-flarge van come Tharsday? What night you say Pring'l gone missin'?'

The chorus again started, variously calling, 'Not Tharsday . . . Wensdy, gal . . . 'leventh . . . same night's you and Johnny was counting them stamps . . . what you'n Johnny bin upter, gal? . . . stow that fer a tale . . . yew let us down, gal . . . come ter think, us han't seen Pring'l that whole week. Not wensdy, tewsdy, mundy . . . '

59

Their voices died away; the tap continued to drip; and then, very slowly Janice Tyler began again.

'That's suthick mighty strange,' she said, 'I now remembers. Johnny and me begin counting stock, like, the night afore that. That must a bin Tuesday night, same's I stand yere. Tooken us two nights. Fust night, Tuesday, knowing as Bestworths was away, Johnny says to me, "Let's go down and have a look," he says. "Get the car out and drive around, like," he says. Well, that's what we done, then. Only when we got down that way we seen a strange van opposight the church. That were druv into Bestworths' garridge or sich-like. You know, where they keeps their lil' ole boat come winter time. Johnny an me reckon that weren't no van of the Bestworths' neether. Us seen that clear, though it were getting nigh on dark. Us got out, quiet like. There that stood. Doors were closed shut at back. Someone were moving about, quiet, inside or summat.'

VII

Mrs Prosit of the King's Road looked shrewdly at Detective Sergeant Simmons, knowing that he was a policeman and not a prospective tenant for one of her furnished rooms. The single gentlemen she provided for were often very dull young men, unlike others she knew of in that somewhat raffish neighbourhood. The Sergeant did not look dull or raffish. He merely seemed exceptionally clean.

He put his bowler hat and neatly rolled umbrella beside his chair and eased the crease of his trousers. He might have been disguised—although not at all heavily disguised—as a junior infantry officer bearing the company commander's condolences to the parent of a missing soldier. She was surprised, however, by his first question: he asked who had painted the half-dozen small landscapes that were on the walls of her office.

'They are my late husband's, Sergeant. He was killed in an air raid. They and this house were all he had to leave me. Perhaps the pictures may one day turn out to be more valuable than the house. If your official enquiries have taken you into the art world, I should value your opinion.'

'They have not yet done so, madam. But these seem,' and he hesitated, 'easier to like than some others I have looked at recently.'

She smiled. 'That is a charming compliment. You said that you have come from Stourminster.' She hesitated. 'A Mr Pringle once lived here. He went to Stourminster about eighteen months ago.'

'Yes, madam, we have heard of him. Indeed, we should be glad of any information about him that you could give.'

'Is it true, then, that he is, er, *missing*?'

'May I ask how you had heard that? I don't think it has been in the newspapers?'

'Well, you see, Mr Pringle wrote to ask me if I could let him his old room during this month. I made the arrangement but he never turned up. I was very surprised.'

'It was unlike him to change his mind?'

'Utterly.'

'Did you know him well, Mrs Prosit?'

'In some ways, yes. He had been with me for ten years, you see. I don't think he had many friends; or if he had, I never saw them here. He was certainly not one to give parties or to try and stow-away a girl-friend overnight. Far from it, I should say. He seemed quite set in his ways, Sergeant: politic, cautious and meticulous—that sort of man, if you take my point.' She wondered whether the Sergeant was looking a bit blank, so she said, 'I am sorry. I am being fanciful.'

'A reliable gentleman?'

'No, I don't think I *should* call him reliable. He was too negative, too feeble to be *relied* on. But once one knew his ways, one found his reactions quite predictable.'

'No doubt an easy tool,' said the Sergeant.

She looked up with a sudden smile. 'I see you do take my point.'

'I don't think you actually told me why you should have thought he might be "missing".'

'Did I not? Well, Sergeant, I told you that he did not turn up here when he was expected; and then you are the second person from Stourminster to come asking recently for his whereabouts.'

'Ah! Do you mind telling me who this other person was?'

'Not in the least. It was a Mr Sherard.'

'Is he a friend of yours?'

'No. I'd never seen him before. I knew *of* him, of course.'

'Mr Sherard is well known?'

'Oh, I think so. I have seen his work reproduced although I have never actually been to one of his exhibitions.'

'Did he explain why he was looking for Mr Pringle?'

'No. Mr Pringle had said that he could be found here during August. I explained that he had never taken up the booking or given any explanation; so Mr Sherard went away again.' She gave the date and time of his visit. 'I was unable to help Mr Sherard, you see.'

'Thank you, it is not important. Could I look at your register of guests before I go? And do you think I could now see the room which Mr Pringle used to occupy?'

She seemed surprised. 'I don't see why not. But all the letting rooms here are very much the same. And there are none of his things here now.' She took some keys. 'However, by all means let us have a look.'

The room was utterly commonplace: fitted basin, built-in wardrobe cupboard, chest of drawers, table, chair and a single-bed with white candlewick spread. Everything was clean, light-coloured and impersonal, with cream paint and freshly buff-distempered walls.

'Has it always looked like this, madam?'

'Why, yes. I re-distemper as often as I think necessary.'

'It's very bright and clean,' he said apologetically, feeling depressed. *He* would not have chosen to smuggle a girl friend across this fluff-free linoleum. Here for ten years, he thought, and then Saint Seb! 'Was he a very tidy gentleman, madam?' Why ask that? Ah! the very tidy cousin! Not that Mr Sherard would live here!

'He didn't accumulate much junk, but he *was* obstinate about where he kept things. He had something in a roll done up in brown paper. He used to prop this up in a corner. Inconvenient, and it marked the wall. So I asked him to keep it in my box room. But he said, no. Eventually he agreed to keep it under the bed. But that wasn't much better, you see: the maid had to keep shifting it when she used the Hoover. However, there it stayed until he left.'

*　*　*

'Well, Sergeant,' said Inspector Glover, 'I hope you haven't run up too many expenses in London? Have you confirmed Sherard's movements? This actress woman now: what's her name, a well-known one?'

'Yes, sir, a Mrs Margaret Capper, sir. I was told that she would be rehearsing at the theatre, so I went along. They were quite agreeable in Shaftsbury Avenue that I should see her. I just had to wait until the end of the scene . . .'

He had sat next to the producer in the darkened stalls. The stage had not been fully lit, so that her face, as she moved about, had been heavily shadowed and so expressionless that she might have been wearing a mask. Her lines had come across as clear as a bell and would have reached, he had supposed, to all parts of the house. At the end of the scene, and before she could leave the stage, the producer had called out, 'That's going to be very good, Meg. Can we go straight to Act Two? Only there's a nice young man here to see you—a Mr Simmons from Stourminster. Come up specially, my dear. Won't go away, either. He has promised not to keep you or to ask you more than one tiny question, O.K?'

She had come forward and peered about, handsome and haggard and rather formidable. He had risen and gone to lean over the orchestra rail. 'Mrs Capper?' he had said.

'Yes? yes? yes?' she had said. 'I don't *think* we have met, Mr Simmons. Not that I can see you at all well. Did I leave something at Stourminster? I *was* there last week.'

'Could I speak in private for a moment?'

'Oh Lord!' she said with a sort of wail. 'I am in the middle of work, my dear man! Can't you just say what it is without making a thing of it?' She made no move and he had to lean further forward. He asked, in a silly-sounding confidential murmur whether she knew a Mr Jack Sherard.

'Jack?' And she could undoubtedly have been heard in the upper gallery. 'I know him very well indeed,' in the same rousing tones, then rising a pitch, 'Why do you ask?'

He murmured, 'Did you see him in London on Wednesday last?'

'I have absolutely no idea who you are, Mr Simmons, and am not, at the moment, madly keen to find out. You did not answer my question, as I remember, and I see no reason why I should answer yours about a very old friend of mine.' A stage hand or two began to hover.

'Is everything o.k., Mrs Capper?' one of them asked.

'Not to bother, Jim. Sweet of you, though . . . Now, sir?'

The Sergeant said, still quietly, 'I am a police officer, madam. Mr Sherard was looking for his cousin.'

She had looked at her watch and turned up her eyes, as if to say, 'God give me patience: you *are* going to make a thing of it after all.' Instead of this she said, 'Very well, Mr Simmons, if you say so. I never knew he *had* a cousin. Damn! I can't *see* you down there in that God-awful sump. If you came up here it might help. There is a pass-door on your right . . . Well, now, my dear man, you don't look so disreputable. Quite the reverse, in fact. Did I see Mr Sherard on Wednesday in London? Actually, no. I slept late that morning. He got his own breakfast and left early. He nearly always does, as a matter of fact. Right?'

'He had, er, spent the night at your, er, flat?'

'Yes, yes, yes. I put him up. Didn't I say?'

And with that he had had to be content . . .

'Um!' said the Inspector. 'Like that, is it? And she makes no bones of it? Hollas it to the reverberate gallery, or whatever?'

'Yes, sir, I felt a bit awkward, sir. But it seems to confirm his story, all right. He was there for the night; and the estate agents say that by ten a.m. he was talking to them in Hammersmith.'

'They knew him?'

'Oh, yes!' He turned to his notes. ' "Mr Sherard is well-known round here. We had been trying to find another studio flat for him before his cousin, Mr Pringle, left our employ." '

'Um! Did they say *why* Pringle left?'

'Actually they had been surprised. Pringle had come to them at the end of the war. They were quite glad to have him, but assumed that he might later be rejoining his father's business. However he stayed on until his father died; then he left. They assumed that he would be taking over and carrying on with the Stourport business. But he sold it.'

'Did he set up elsewhere in the same line?'

'No sir. He came to Saint Sebastian and did absolutely nothing for eighteen months. It *is* odd.'

'Not nearly as odd, Sergeant, as getting himself crammed into a pew in a disused church, which he had crawled about in as a kid with his Sherard cousin. Well, you've confirmed Sherard's movements in London; and I don't see that you can have run up any out-of-the-way expenses there, unless you had to buy a Munnings for us at the Cornford Gallery. Let's hear all about it.'

'I confirmed that Mr Sherard had been there as well, sir. But . . . er, possible witness there, sir: lunch expenses, sir.' He coloured.

'We had better hear about that, my lad.'

*   *   *

The sergeant had looked at the papers to see what would be showing at the gallery and had noted, 'BIRETTA/ Recent Sculpture/ until September 11.' Another week to run.

When he had walked into the Gallery, however, there was apparently nothing but unoccupied stands; and there had been no one about. Or so he had thought until an extremely pretty girl came up from the basement crossly cramming something into a handbag. She was carrying gloves and wore a fetching black apache cap. Intent upon holding a moment of time he had walked towards her.

'Er, my name is Simmons,' he had said.

'Good morning, Mr Simmons.' Her frown was replaced by a dimple. Crumbs! he had thought, feeling faint.

'It's quite all right, Mr Simmons. What can I do for you? I'm not going out just at the moment. It's just that I was waiting to be relieved for lunch and felt so ravenous, I couldn't ... I'm so sorry: I interrupted you. Did you want to see Mr Mallender? Only I'm afraid he's in Paris. Or was it about a Biretta?'

' "About a *biretta*"?' he said, having already forgotten the ostensible purpose of the exhibition. He looked round blankly at unoccupied chromium-plated stands seemingly prepared for damn-all. She began to giggle delightfully and he was enchanted.

'If you didn't get to last year's *Biennale*,' she said, 'you might not have seen his work before. This is the first time he has shown over here ... we were lucky to get him, actually.'

'He's an, er, *sculptor*?' And he blushed.

She decided that he was really rather sweet, noticing a golden down on his cheekbones: his silk-straight fair hair had been flattened by his bowler hat and curled slightly over his ears. He was certainly not in the gallery business. Or a critic? Except, perhaps, writing for some very new undergraduate magazine? He was not tall—just above her own height—but the way he stood suggested that he might be able to move very quickly . . .

She, too, felt herself blushing, and bent to open a drawer in her desk where she fortunately found a file of press-cuttings. She demurely offered these.

After glancing at them he realised that he was among *exhibits*, no less. 'Metal Sculpture by Biretta at the Cornford', said a headline; 'Comic Strip!' said another. 'Tube-root of Zero!' said the *Express*; 'Reductio ad . . . ?' asked the *Telegraph*. Robert Melville, in *The New Statesman*, began with, ' "But where's the bloody horse?" '

Encouraged by the latter, he said, 'It's very simplified and restrained. I see.'

'Oh, it is,' she admitted; and his heart turned over at the reappearance of the dimple.

'Is there a name for this kind of work?' he asked.

'Actually, it's known as "Minimal",' she said gravely.

Well, he consoled himself: *de minimis*,* and I am the Law. I don't have to concern myself with such things. He smiled at her, 'Could you tell me, please, would Mr Sherard's pictures be "minimal"?'

'Oh, I don't think so. Jack Sherard? Well, he's more like Mark Rothko, sort of? Quite a lot goes on in his pictures. Only two or three patches of colour; but he doesn't just show blank canvases, if you see what I mean?'

'Is that allowed? Blank canvases, I mean.'

'Well, it's done, you know. Quite often. Do you know Mr Sherard, then?'

'We have met,' he said vaguely. Then, 'He was showing me some of his latest last week as a matter of fact. He said he had been up to see Mr Mallender.'

'Oh, he had. He was here last Wednesday and was with Mr Mallender for about an hour. Actually he arrived just as

*de minimis non curat lex, the law does not bother with trifles.

68

I had got *back* from lunch.' She looked at her watch. 'Damn this bitch!'

'As a matter of interest,' he said, 'I was wondering if you could tell me something about Mr Sherard and his work. That is, if it wouldn't be a bore talking shop. Er, I must get back to the country'—ah, yes, she thought—'and I might not have time to call back here after lunch. Er, would it be possible for you to have lunch with me—that is, if you can get away?'

She brightened, 'I shall be delighted; and it is very kind of you to suggest it. This more than softens the blow dealt by this bloody woman I am waiting for. I can see that you are faint with hunger. I'll give her five more minutes and then we'll lock up and go.'

'Well, that's all right then, and thank you very much. There will be no hurry as far as I am concerned. But you'll have to steer my footsteps. You might say that my knowledge of where to eat round here is, er, Minimal . . .'

VIII

ON THE DAY that Sergeant Simmons was making his enquiries in London Frank Fenwick called on old Mr Poleyn
at Stourminster. He was shown into a study looking on to the
Cathedral close.

'My very dear sir,' said Mr Poleyn, unable to rise, 'how
kind of you to call! I am extremely sorry not to have kept my
appointment with you yesterday at Saint Sebastian Sibling.
And I was most distressed to learn of the horrible trouble you
and the vicar ran into when you got there. Dear me! Extraordinary! Dear me! But *I* shouldn't have been much help.
Under those circumstances I fear that my presence would
only have been an extra embarrassment.'

Mr Fenwick trusted that Mr Poleyn was beginning to
recover from his lumbago and would be able to look at Saint
Sebastian later. 'But I had the advantage of the admirable
report you made for Canon Template nearly fifty years ago.
I wonder if you could cast your mind back to the early years
of your practice. I have an idea that some explanation of
what has just happened may lie in the not too distant past.'

'How very interesting, my dear sir. I wish more of us
would look for such rational explanations of present-day
consequences. It *was* early in my practice, as you say, but I
remember that time more clearly, I think, than much that
has happened since. They are dear dead days to me. "Days,"
as Wordsworth says, that were "as long as twenty days are
now." Well, sir, and how can I help you?'

'Saint Sebastian village is now sadly shrunk. Even so, I can't imagine that it was ever populous. Its church is very small.'

'Certainly. But in Canon Template's time, it was in very good nick, as I believe they say nowadays.' He made a little bob in Mr Fenwick's direction. 'The roof was sound; and in spite of its watery situation, there was no rising damp. It was Canon Template, incidentally, who put in the heating system. That must have helped.'

'You mentioned a reredos, or rather, a painting of Our Lady.'

'Yes, I don't think you could call it a reredos. At that time there was an embroidered dorsal and riddels laced to a rail. This picture was well above, fixed to the wall; quite a way up—too high, really. It was in rather a good frame. At any rate the frame suited the picture.'

'Sir Francis tells me that this picture was probably one that had been presented by the Sibthorps. Was it old?'

'I think it must have been. I advised the Canon to take expert opinion. I have since read of similar. I remember this one so clearly because it was an odd thing to find over an altar in an Anglican village church. It was a black Madonna!'

' "A *black* Madonna?" How extraordinary! And where would the Sibthorps have found such a thing? Africa? South India? Or what about Goa? It was Portuguese, perhaps?'

'It *might* have been Portuguese. A most interesting suggestion, my dear sir. It was certainly not African. You see, it *was* baroque.'

He rubbed his hands delightedly, as though Frank Fenwick had delicately placed a late cut to the boundary between first and second slip.

'Quite definitely baroque. But Goanese? I *think*, I *think* it came from somewhere quite else. I had better describe it.'

'Please do.'

71

'It was not large: about three foot high and most delicately painted. The Virgin was shown standing, holding the Christ Child on her left arm. Both were in embroidered copes, crowned and with haloes. So far normal enough, my dear sir, but she was black.'

'Verdigris-dark? Byzantine?'

'No, no. I take your point.' He bobbed. 'In many of the Byzantine ikons the flesh colour *is*, or has become, dark from being painted on copper. Byzantine faces also tend to be long, even emaciated. But in the picture I am talking about Our Lady's features were full, almost plump. But very, very beautiful, with a straight nose and a very delicate, straight mouth. Nothing negroid in spite of the dark skin. You see, the Holy Child, by contrast, was conspicuously fair. The demarcation must have been quite deliberate, my dear sir. *Ecce ancilla Domini?*'*

'Of course, and the artist?'

'Ah, who shall say? Almost certainly a Latin-American. Perhaps a Peruvian? As I expect you know, lay brothers in the Jesuit missions, there, painted such images to appeal to and involve the "Indians" who filled their churches. Understandable, wouldn't you say? Most of these pictures have now been lost. Has this one also disappeared?'

'Well, it's no longer in that place, Mr Poleyn.'

'Ah! It might indeed have been at risk. The good Canon Template was followed by a Reverend James Tasker, a priest more likely to have swept than to have garnished a sanctuary.'

'The Ten Commandments now hang there.'

'Indeed. Then I really do feel that we are in Tasker territory, where a "likeness of anything that is in the heaven above" would not be tolerated. Eh? De-ar me! How very sad! I only hope that he did not consign our picture to the

* 'Behold the handmaid of the Lord.'

72

Thumbelow Drain, which washes its walls on the southern side.' He sniffed. 'But I am sure, my dear sir, that if the Reverend James destroyed the image he would have found some useful purpose for the frame: it had garnets in it.'

'Mr Tasker must have left the diocese before my time?'

'I suppose so. He was inclined to wage war on his parishioners, which is not what bishops like best in their clergy. The living is now combined with Saint Osyth, I believe. I don't think I have met the present incumbent.'

'It's a Mr Chew. But of course you have been in correspondence. He and I were talking about the big house opposite the church at Saint Sebastian. Could you say how it came to be built?'

'Ah, yes. For a Mr Mostyn Pringle. He was an oddity. But he had the sense to employ a good architect of an Annesley Voyseyish or Mackmurdoish kind, if you know what I mean?'

'Yes, I think so: my wife said it might have been built by the young Bosinney, who . . .'

'Almost the very touch, my dear sir. Excellent! Excellent! But not quite. Mostyn Pringle was no Soames Forsyte. Mostyn would have asked for something more home-spun, a suggestion of sack-cloth, eh?'

'The house looks very well-built.'

'Undoubtedly. Nothing out-at-elbows. No rags. The very best sack-cloth and the merest sprinkling of well-screened ashes. Use nothing but honest materials and show how you use them. Of course that is always very expensive; but in those days there was money about. Mostyn Pringle was great on Fabian Society Summer Schools—wore Norfolk suits and went in for bird-watching. He published a book on grebes at his own expense. Otherwise he was bone-idle. He married money: a Miss Honor Bolton from the Potteries. As Saint Paul assuredly did not say: it is better to marry than to earn. Ahem!' He made another placatory bob. 'She died soon after the son, Reginald, was born. Mostyn was a prig. He had the sort of principles to which he sacrificed anyone else's rather than his own convenience. For example, in deference to the Arts and Crafts movement he sent his own motherless son to some ghastly school where all they taught was wicker-work. With no education to speak of, he ended up, as an ex-officer after the 1914 war, selling houses in Stourport, poor fellow. A bruised reed, I fear.'

'It will have been Reginald Pringle's son whose body I found?'

'Dear me, yes! Of course, Thomas! That boy's mother was a well-connected Irish gal. It's a mystery how she put up with the Pringles in spite of their money. This gal, if you please, on her marriage to master Reginald, was expected to set up home with her husband in the same house as the old man. Not that the house wasn't big enough. Well, that's where Thomas Pringle was born, sometime during the 1914 war.'

'And what happened to the boy?'

'Let me see. I never met Thomas. Used to hear about him. I am told that he too became a reed shaken with the wind. Hardly surprising, perhaps. His rich egalitarian grandfather had him sent to the village school.'

'Well, come. He might have fared worse, Mr Poleyn, after what you said about wicker-work. The boy would at least have been efficiently drilled in script and ciphering.'

'That's as may be. From my information Thomas became sly, devious and mean-minded. But if he was the last of the Pringles there is probably still a lot of money to go some-where.'

'The police say that Thomas Pringle never married.'

'Ah! Their race is run. A sad and uneventful history . . .' He cautiously tried to stand, but settled back with a groan. 'Alas,' he said, 'I can in no wise lift up myself. You must

74

forgive me, my dear sir. Perhaps, soon, I may be able to join you at Saint Sebastian's church. As it is, I am afraid that I have been singularly unhelpful.'

'On the contrary . . .'

'Well, I have remembered the picture—black, my dear sir, but definitely comely.'

'Mr Poleyn, believe me. I really am grateful. Moreover, if you will allow me, I shall advise the police to consult you. I think you have indicated a possible line of enquiry.'

IX

THE INQUEST at Stourminster on the body of Thomas Pringle decided that he had met his death by a blow at the base of the skull. The jury, as directed by the Coroner, was unable to decide how or by whom the blow had been struck, or how the body came to be bundled into a pew of the church. The Coroner then adjourned further discussion to allow the police time to investigate these teasing questions. Before adjournment he had also refused to add the rider, suggested by one juryman, to the effect that parish clergy should not allow their churches to be used for such goings on.

Jack Sherard had given evidence of identity. Afterwards Detective Chief Superintendent Quill invited him to police headquarters round the corner: there were still a few questions that needed an answer. Jack Sherard was entirely at his service, and presently found himself not uncomfortably facing the light in the Superindendent's office. Behind him, Sergeant Simmons's blond head was lowered over a note book.

Jack wore a suit of grey herring-bone tweed with a blue viyella shirt and a black knitted silk tie. This was unexceptionable for the occasion but seemed dauntingly chic. The Superintendent eyed him carefully: he doubted if this was the ornament of a meek and quiet spirit.

'Mr Sherard,' he said, 'you were very helpful when we arrived on the scene of what must now be rightly dealt with as homicide. I cannot tell you when this inquest will be resumed or whether you may be further required in that connection; but may I ask about your immediate plans?'

'Well, Chief Superintendent, if there is no further official business to detain me, I shall move back to London. As you know, I shall be involved there with my exhibition which opens in ten days' time. I should be honoured if you can accept an invitation for the Private View, which will be on a Tuesday; but can scarcely expect that you would be free.'

'That is extremely kind of you, sir. I cannot, indeed, know what my commitments will be ten days from now. And where shall you be saying in London?'

'Oh, Mrs Capper has kindly offered to put me up.'

'At the same Notting Hill address?'

'Certainly.'

'May I ask you to get in touch with the local police should you change your plans? I might need to consult you again.'

'Well, I suppose so.'

'Mr Sherard, when you were last helping us you mentioned a previous incident in this same church at Saint Sebastian Sibling. It was connected with your late cousin and the present village shopkeeper.'

There was no reply. Jack continued to look at his questioner.

'If I may say so,' said Quill, 'it was an odd tale.'

Again there was no reply. The Superintendent waited with a mixture of amusement and annoyance. This bloke answers by the book. He put a direct question. 'Do you agree that it may have seemed an odd tale?'

'Remembrance of things past, Superintendent, can seem odd, no doubt. However, I am no Marcel Proust. All this happened nearly fifty years ago. After I had recently identified my cousin's body in the churchyard, you asked me whether I had ever before been *inside* the church. I thought that I had better answer your question, and since it concerned my childhood I explained the circumstances of my visit. I may not have remembered all the details. I repeat, I am no Marcel Proust. I haven't what I believe is known as "total recall". Does it matter?'

'You told me a very great deal, sir. I thought it curiously vivid. The oddness of the circumstances perhaps do not concern me. I wondered whether you can now remember what the place looked like when you were a child?'

'Tolerably well: a plain and light interior with clear glass windows. And there were those great box pews. I don't remember a pulpit or lectern. There may have been such furniture, but I never attended a service, you see. It could be said that my cousin and I were among those who used to creep and intrude and climb into the fold . . .'

'I understand, sir. I was wondering if you could remember what the east end of the church was like, its chancel or whatever?'

'Oh, Lord, yes! Though I may speak with the hindsight, not of childish innocence, but of an interested visitor of old buildings. The front pews just stopped. There was no division or crossing, no arch or chancel-steps; and your "east end" was just a wall with the altar table against it. Oh, yes, and above that was hung an old picture. And a very odd one, too.'

'Ah! A picture? Not a list of the Commandments?'

'Certainly not. There would have been nothing odd about that, I suppose?'

'Well, a picture: how was it odd?'

'I'd better be careful or I shall say what I *think* may have been there. For instance, I now suppose that it was a madonna and child. But I don't remember a child: only the standing figure of a woman; and her face was black. Quite, quite black!'

'Did this seem frightening?'

'Not in the least. It was probably very lovely. But definitely black.'

78

'This picture was behind the altar?'

'Yes. Or rather, on the wall above it: much too high, as I should probably think now—skied, in fact. And there were two stone cherub heads somewhere near the ceiling. Only, at this remove, I can't tell you whether they would have been *trompe l'œil* (that is, painted in mock relief) or actual carved heads in stone . . . May I ask why you want to know all this?'

'That is remarkably detailed, sir. And helpful. It ties up with another description of the church at about that time. We don't know whether the madonna painting can be connected with this other business; but the painting is no longer there.'

'That does not surprise me, Superintendent: I should be surprised if it were.'

'Valuable?'

'Probably. I, for one, would like to see it again.'

'Now sir, to come to more personal business: we learn that Sparrows Bank here hold your late cousin's Will, and that you are the sole beneficiary.'

'Yes.'

'Did you know that before his death?'

'No.'

'Are you surprised?'

'Not really. He had no other next of kin. But I have never been in his confidence, and he certainly never told me that he had made this Will.'

'Forgive me if my questions seem impertinent, but . . .'

'I take it that by "impertinent" you do *not* mean irrelevant?'

'No, indeed, and thank you, sir.'

'Ask away, Chief Superintendent.'

'Is the estate large?'

'I have yet to learn the details. His grandfather must have been fairly rich.'

79

'As next of kin, does your indifference mean that you are not in need of money?'

'One is always in need of money, is one not? But my needs at present are not pressing.'

'This forthcoming exhibition?'

'Neither here nor there. It is not a "selling" gallery—not directly, that is. Nor is the show an expense to me. Since I can guess, I think, the drift of your questions, let me say that I have a small private income, am reasonably successful in my profession, am unmarried and no more willing than most to pay punitive income tax.'

'Who owns the large house by the church?'

'I have no idea, Chief Superintendent.'

(The note-taking Sergeant Simmons wondered why the Chief Superintendent was keeping the bowling well outside the off-stump: but the questions would certainly be best left alone by a cautious batsman at this stage of the innings.)

'Have you been back to see the house during your recent stay? . . . You knew it as a child.'

'That is true, of course.'

'What is true, Mr Sherard?'

'That I knew the house as a child.' (Ah, padding-up to a turning ball.)

'Have you seen it since?'

'I saw the outside when your Inspector drove me down to the church.'

'Did you notice the garage (or more strictly speaking, car-port) at the side of the house?'

'No.' (A straight ball. He is making him play them.)

'Are you an observant man, Mr Sherard?'

'I suppose I am as observant as most other professional painters, which means that I am normally tolerably noticing. But on this occasion your Inspector was in a bit of a taking and I was trying to pay him attention. He wanted to prepare me for what I was about to be shown, and I was not much relishing the prospect. If I noticed what you call a car-port at the side of that house, I do not now remember doing so, Superintendent.' (Four leg byes.)

'You run two motor cars, Mr Sherard?' (The super is signifying his intention of bowling round the wicket.)

'I have a van for my pictures. But when I got to Stour-minster I hired a small Austin as a runabout.'

'Did you always keep your van outside the old school building where you worked?'

'Yes.'

'Invariably?'

There was a pause. 'I certainly cannot remember seeing it moved off the verge until your driver kindly took me in it up to London.'

'Did you ever lend it to anyone or offer to do so while you were down here?'

'No.'

'Would it surprise you to know, Mr Sherard, that a van like yours was seen one night, in the car-port of that house where you stayed as a child?'

'Yes.'

'It would surprise you, you say? Can you account for it?' (A quicker one on the leg peg.)

'Well, what am I expected to say to that?' He smiled. 'I have no means of knowing what are the dark goings on during summer nights at Saint Sebastian. I have always left the place before half past six. I used to drive back every evening to my hotel at Stourminster.' (Two runs past fine leg.)

'Would you agree that your van is rather distinctive?'

'Perhaps. It is not unique. It is of a kind used by shop-fitters and glaziers. One of my picture dealers has one like it.' (Sergeant Simmons looked up.)

'Would that be the Cornford Gallery?' Quill asked.

'Well, yes, since you mention it. These vans are useful for taking pictures about.' (The sergeant, however, had given up his imaginary score card. He was thinking of the bliss to be travelling as police escort of some minimal Biretta, in the back of a van with a dark-haired girl in an apache cap.)

'Very well, sir. As you say, there are other vans on the road. Do you know where your own was on the nights of Tuesday and Wednesday, the tenth and eleventh of August this year?'

Jack Sherard looked at his pocket diary. 'Yes, I certainly know where *my* van was on those two nights. It was in the yard behind my old studio building in London. The eleventh was the night before I came down here. It was all packed up and ready for the journey.'

'Thank you, I don't think there are any other questions. Oh yes, you had written to your cousin confirming the time of your arrival on the twelfth?'

'Certainly.'

'Was this the letter?' and keeping his thumb over the 'A' on the transparent envelope, he showed the exhibit.

'Yes, where did you find it . . . ? In the clothes that he was wearing when he was killed? Poor chap! How awful! I think that must be the only thing I have ever written to him in my life. So he knew exactly when I was coming. This must show, Chief Superintendent that he was dead before I got here . . .'

'Well, sir, it might and it mightn't.' The Sergeant's head came up to watch the effect when exhibit 'B' should be produced. But instead there was a pause. Then Quill said, 'I have no other question at the moment, Mr Sherard.'

X

Mr Chew was in Stourminster on Trustee business. King Sigebert's Charity of Elvers End had once been administered by a Collegiate Body of Clerks Regular to distribute money among seamen's widows of pious life for the education of such of their children of school age as had been born at Elvers End or otherwise in the Soke of Domcaister.

The bishop had appointed Trustees to succeed for this purpose since the Chapter House at Elvers End, together with the greater part of that parish had long since been swept away by the sea, thereby illustrating the motto that the foundation had taken, although perhaps not with this precise event in mind, from Hebrews xiii 14, *non habemus hic manentem civitatem*.* The Trustees now met at Stourminster.

The present meeting had been brief since the sole applicant had been a deserving woman with three young daughters and an older boy who was to be entered at Stourport Grammar School. After the Trustees had risen, Mr Chew asked for a word with Frank Fenwick. The latter was able to give news of old Mr Poleyn's recovery. They were able, therefore, to fix a date for their next visit to Saint Sebastian.

'Ah, yes!' said Mr Chew, 'that last visit of ours was a week ago, wasn't it? More? Dear me! That was most—well, it was most un-*four*-chinit! . . . I have not heard . . . ?'

'Inspector Glover of the Stourminster C.I.D. does not think they need keep the church under police seal any

*For here we have no continuing city.

longer. That roof-fall in the south porch was due to rotten timber. The lead had been stolen from it a long time ago. The broken chancel door has been boarded up, but *we* can get in as soon as we may wish.'

'Ah, that is good! Very good! . . .'

'That school building, Chew, is not our responsibility, but I don't think the police need *that* any longer. I expect that they can pursue future enquiries more conveniently from their own headquarters.'

'Does that mean that the village is no longer under, um?'

'I don't know what it means, Chew. Your guess would be as good as mine, since you probably know what questions the police have been asking, and whether they have finished with them at Saint Sebastian.'

'I rather think they have, Canon. And that would be the best news, do you not think? Dear me! They may want to talk to the Bestworths when they get back from their sailing holiday. I don't suppose those worthy people can tell them much. "Routine enquiries" was the word. I hope otherwise that they will find a line to follow that leads them much further afield than my parish. It would be most un-*fourchinit* if it turned out otherwise. This, er, other gentleman— artist of a sort, who . . .'

'Mr Sherard?'

'Ah! Just so! That's the name! He has, er, gone?'

'He is in London, Chew. He has an exhibition coming on, you may remember.'

'Oh, would he attach importance to that, just now?'

'I expect so, Chew. It is his vocation, you know.'

'Dear me! I suppose it may be. I was just, er, wondering about his relationship with that other—Mr Pringle, poor fellow. What happens next about that?'

'A natural question, Chew. He was your parishioner, of course. I think, perhaps, now that the inquest is over—or adjourned—you should ask the police. This Mr Sherard is next of kin, you see. The police will arrange with him about the funeral. Sherard *might* suggest your church, but would want to avoid any fuss. I am sure he will do the proper thing. He will turn up for it, wherever it may be.'

'Oh dear! Somehow I hadn't thought of him . . . would he really be an, er, *executor*, Canon?'

'I rather think so, for what it amounts to.'

'Could I perhaps seek your advice? A rather strange situation has arisen.' Mr Chew explained about the 'daub' that Pringle had asked him to look after at the vicarage. 'You see, Canon, when poor Pringle did not turn up again, I showed this, er, object to his cousin.'

'Well, Chew, that was sensible under the circumstances. What did Sherard say?'

There was a pause. Then, 'Well, you know, my wife and I thought this strange attempt at a picture had been one of Pringle's own efforts and that he might have been shy of leaving it about in his own house to be seen by a real artist like this cousin, who was coming to stay. But Sherard said that he actually recognised its authorship, and he mentioned the artist's name. I can't remember what it was, but I'll tell you in a moment. I've had a letter about it. Anyway, the name meant nothing to me or my wife . . . and then, of course, with poor Mr Pringle dying, we wondered what to do with the rubbishy thing. It was up in our box room, loosely tacked to a bit of board.'

Frank Fenwick looked worried, 'Is it still . . . ?'

'And then, you see, this Mr Sherard had also gone back to London. We, er, didn't know what to do . . .'

'Have you still . . . ?'

'Well, actually, there has been this unexpected letter from Mr Sherard in London. It arrived the day before yesterday.' He handed over a typewritten letter with 'from J. Sherard, c/o Mrs M. Capper' appearing over the engraved Notting Hill heading of the writing paper. It was addressed formally to 'The Vicar, Saint Osyth Sibling.'

Dear Mr Chew,

You will remember that Mrs Capper and I met you in my late cousin Thomas Pringle's house at Saint Sebastian some time before his death had been suspected, let alone discovered. You asked us both to your vicarage to see a canvas that my cousin had left in your safe-keeping. I recognised this as a valuable painting (which I had once seen) by the french artist, E. Vuillard.

It seems that I am to be the sole beneficiary of my cousin's Will and that this painting, which you still hold, will come to me. May I therefore ask you to take care of it until I shall have got my new exhibition open on September 14. I shall, in the mean time, be more than willing to pay to you, or to any worthy cause you might name, a small sum in token of my appreciation of your continuing custody. But if there is any difficulty or inconvenience about this, please say.

Yours faithfully,

J. Sherard

Frank Fenwick noted the precise, almost pernickety language. Correct! But correct! Yet somehow, he thought, he did not like Mr Sherard. The lines of Martial, so memorably transferred in English to the unfortunate Doctor Fell, seemed to apply. Nevertheless, he felt vaguely alarmed on his colleague's behalf.

'Well, Chew, this Mr Sherard seems to be making sure that you go on looking after his picture, which he—how does it go?—"left in your safekeeping", eh?'

Mr Chew looked unhappy. 'Well, of course,' he said,

'it never occurred to me . . . would a picture by this, er . . . ?'

'Vuillard?'

'Yes, *would* it be valuable as he suggests?'

'At a guess, and not having seen it, I would say that it might fetch thirty or fifty thousand pounds . . .'

A look of such utter desolation passed over Mr Chew's face—a face seldom marked by strong emotion—that Frank Fenwick turned away in pity, quite unable to ask the one question that mattered. They were in the upper room of a one-time Victorian mansion which now housed the diocesan offices. They both stared down, through a plate glass bay window, at an expanse of lawn between the house and a great copper beech tree. As the silence continued, a door at the back of the room opened and a secretary looked in to collect any abandoned order-papers. But seeing the two clergymen still in commune, she silently withdrew. At last, appalled by the unfairness of what he supposed might have happened, Frank Fenwick said, 'I'm afraid each of us is out of his depth, Chew, and I won't ask any more questions. But since you sought my advice, I should take that letter to police head-quarters in Mixen Street and show it to Detective Chief Superintendent Quill. I think it may have considerable bearing on things that are well outside our control. Quill is a very intelligent officer.'

There was an unhappy silence. Fenwick continued to speak, 'You are distressed, perhaps, about the extraordinary situation into which we have both been pressed. I will come with you, if you wish. I know Quill quite well.'

Mr Chew continued to stare out of the window. It occurred to the other that Chew had perhaps not heard a word of what had been said since he merely continued to move his head from side to side. But eventually Chew turned and, perhaps unseeingly, picked his way between the heavy chairs that had been pushed back from the table. He left the room.

XI

THE CHIEF SUPERINTENDENT greatly admired Canon Fenwick and had sometimes been glad to discuss a police case with him. But the place where Pringle's dead body had been found was not in the Canon's parish; and the police could not expect from him any out-of-the-way local knowledge to help them.

For that matter the Chief Superintendent did not expect locals to be involved. He had uncovered a surprising amount of unedifying activity in the flat Sibling furlongs. None, however, seemed to point to a homicide such as he was investigating. Although the first suggestion to have come up was wide of the mark, namely that there had been an attempt to conceal a road accident, the Chief Superintendent by no means ruled out an unplanned killing by some comparative stranger.

But why in a disused church? He did not think the body had just been dumped there. He thought it likely that the victim had been a party to the breaking and entering. Why, therefore, after the church had been closed for so long, should anyone now want to get inside?

Well, the parsons had needed to, for their own good reasons. And there are many good reasons for others to enter old churches. But he could think of no respectable reason for forcing an entry. Was there anything in the church worth stealing? Or destroying? Lead had been taken from the porch, and this suggested a foray from a town where such loot would be disposable. The more recent break-in had been done with an instrument brought for the purpose: perhaps on information known to those involved. Recent information?

Pringle and his cousin, however tenuously they might be connected with the village by past association, were both essentially strangers and newcomers. Both were Londoners. Would London be the great anonymous bully of Sebastian's shrinking silences, reaching to strike down its own emissaries in locked and deserted places?

Should he now seek the assistance of Scotland Yard? Or was there still time to go back to the Reverend Frank Fenwick, M.C., M.A.? For at this gentleman's instigation relevant information had already been provided unexpectedly by at least two persons: the elderly and lumbar-racked Stourminster architect and the scarcely coherent vicar. The information of each was curiously similar. Two quite separate works of art—and potentially valuable—had apparently gone adrift in the Saint Sebastian backwaters.

Who in the Stour Siblings would know a Teniers from a Tissot? Well, an artist might; and an artist had duly turned up, pat. If artist he really were? What was the rather sophisticated phrase Quill had found himself using about the chap's work? *Tachisme?* That was it! Tatty *tachisme*, um!

The Chief Constable, with an entirely new field of enquiry before him and an interesting one, had suggested to his Detective Chief Superintendent that, before tangling with the arcana of London art experts, he again talk over the case with his old friend the Canon. And here Quill was, in the Canon's study, explaining that the police could not credit village mayhem with responsibility for Thomas Pringle's death.

'I am greatly relieved to hear you say so,' said Frank Fenwick, 'and Mr Chew will be relieved also. Not that it makes the murder itself less wicked. Have you kept it so far from the Press?'

'We've had very little to release, and they don't seem interested in this Mr Sherard.'

'Should they be, Quill?'

'Well, sir, he gets the money; and that's not to be sneezed at. The red paper-seal you mentioned may have come off a legal document?'

'Are you teasing me with the suggestion that there was a fight over title deeds or a tussle in the chancel over the dead man's last Will and Testament?'

'Not really, sir. It might have come off a Will, certainly, but not from Thomas Pringle's, as deposited at Sparrow's Bank. That's quite intact.'

'Well, I can't help you, then. These little paper discs are not only toys for lawyers to play with. Dealers put them on picture-frames to show that an artist's work has been sold.'

'Artists again!'

'Again? I can see no reason why Pringle, his assailant, or that bit of paper should have been in that church. Do you know who broke open the chancel door?'

'We think so. It was done with a jemmy or such-like.'

'Dear me! That sounds alarmingly criminal! Even I have heard of a jemmy.'

'A jemmy need not be criminal, although it's undoubtedly handy for breaking and entering. It's a bent piece of steel bar with a claw at one end and a chisel point at the other. A crowbar is straight and more than a yard long. Then it's a case-opener, you see—innocent enough for those used to handling things in packing cases.'

'Did the late Thomas Pringle deal in such wares?'

'Not that we know, sir. His cousin, the artist, may well have done.'

'You are working back to Mr Sherard. But the two of them never met down here, did they, Quill?'

'Well, sir, we can't be sure. We are now inclined to think

that Mr Sherard arrived at Saint Sebastian Sibling a day or two sooner than he has so far admitted.'

*   *   *

'You must admit, Quill,' said Frank Fenwick when the Chief Superintendent had finished, 'there is no direct evidence against Sherard. Are you even sure that it was *his* van that was seen here before his "actual" arrival? What your witnesses later knew to have been his van stood for a week or two on the Green. They say the one they saw earlier was "like" it. Apart from this they don't exactly back each other up, do they? The postmaster says he saw a van "past midnight under a tree". Now there's only one tree down there and it's about a hundred yards from the Green, and almost a mile from where the postwoman saw a van "early", opposite the church. I know, if there ever was a van, it could easily have moved a mile between early Tuesday night and early Wednesday morning. But your two witnesses don't claim to have been together.'

'My trouble is, sir, that I think they were together. She says that she could hear people moving about inside the van like, ahem, a courting couple. No voices, er, movements. She felt a delicacy in getting any closer. From what you might call general knowledge locally I think this postmaster and postwoman were a courting couple themselves. I suppose I shouldn't use the word "courting" since each party is otherwise well and truly married, sir.'

' "Adultery" is the word you need, Quill.'

'Yes, sir.'

'Not going to be star witnesses, eh?'

'Afraid not, sir.'

' "And what, after all, have these sordid matters to do with my client?" '

'Fair enough, sir.'

'A van with living occupants, who were heard but not seen, is reported to have been parked in that boat-house. I have only seen the place by daylight when I backed my own car into it. Now, I am reminded of something, although I don't know what it is at the moment. Perhaps it will come back to me later. Have the Bestworths said anything, now they're back?'

'They don't give Janice Tyler much of a character. She used to "do" for them, but they got rid of her. She cast a roving eye at their son, Jimmy. She is what I might describe as careless and good natured.'

'And the Bestworths?'

'We-ell, they are not what I would call particularly good-natured, sir. Keep themselves to themselves. I am told they are not at all interested in the neighbourhood. It beats me why they ever settled there. I'm also told that they have taken against your colleague, Mr Chew.'

'Oh? What has he done or not done?'

'He once brought over his Osyth congregation, such as it is, for a service at Saint Sebs.'

'Of course. There are those at Saint S. who never come to their only working church at Saint O; so he brought Saint Osyth with him to Saint Seb. What's the trouble?'

'Holding an open air service, sir! *Churches* are meant for such things. Um?'

'Yes, I know the argument, Quill. A character in a Graham Greene novel—*A Burnt Out Case* I think it was—after saying that men have prayed in prisons and slums, points out that suitable surroundings for prayer seem only to be demanded by the middle classes.'

'I see what you mean, sir.'

*　　*　　*

'I now remember, Quill, what I wanted to tell you about a movement I heard in that car-port.'

'At the house opposite the Saint Seb church?'

'Yes. Your postwoman saw a van drawn up there and thought she heard people moving about inside it.'

'Yes, she did.'

'Well, the open sides of that place are draped in polythene sheets. When I got back after leaving my own car there I thought that someone was moving about under the chassis. Then I realised that the stirring and shifting sound came from those polythene things backing and filling with air currents. It's an eery sound: it might well frighten anyone in the dark. The point is this: even if your witness did see a van there, it could have been quite unoccupied.'

'Thank you, sir. We have established that no one was in the house. It is likely that if a van had been left there, the party concerned would have been in the church.'

'And I can think of no other reason for leaving a car. No one who wanted to get to the church would dream of driving over those stepping stones. Leave the car; go on foot.'

'Footmarks in the church, sir: one set was deceased's, the other, small footed, seems to have been his attacker's. Neither set points to Sherard, who has long narrow feet. Whose are the small ones?'

'Man's? woman's? child's?'

'Man's, I should think, sir . . .'

'Well, wouldn't it be safer to look for someone else who might have been with Pringle, rather than to try to cram the cousin's big feet into small shoes? Also, any van outside may have held a canoodling couple or been unoccupied. Either way it could have nothing to do with the case?'

'The same van, sir, innocent or suspicious, may have been seen later near the Green. Or when Plump realised that his floozie had blurted out that she had been so near the incident on the fatal night, he may have made up the second parking place to remove himself from awkward questioning. The Green is much nearer his shop than the church is.'

'All right, Quill. To summarise, let us admit that the second set of footprints at the scene of the crime may be the murderer's but cannot be Sherard's; and also that no direct evidence points to Sherard being seen in person that night by anyone at all. Next, apart from your two differing witnesses, who severally or together may or may not have seen some sort of van, no one else in the village saw anything remotely relevant. Everyone was either watching television or in bed. You tell me it was not a busy night at the pub: only four locals used it, and these, reasonably or passably sober, came in and out by the side facing away from Church Lane. The only testifiable first time that Sherard arrived in Saint Sebastian would be midday on Thursday the twelfth of August.'

'That is fair enough, sir. Sherard, of course, freely admits writing the letter confirming his intended arrival on the twelfth. He wrote it on August the third. But then, sir, on the ninth, which was the Monday (the day before we think Pringle was killed) Sherard seems to have written to his cousin again, undertaking to be with him "Tuesday, p.m." and leaving him "to make all necessary arrangements". Whatever that means . . .'

'And does Mr Sherard "freely admit" writing the second letter? If so, he can presumably explain what he meant?'

There was a silence. Then, 'Mr Sherard doesn't yet know that we hold this second letter, Canon. I judged it better to wait before putting it to him . . .'

'Well, you know your own business best, Quill . . .' Silence continued. 'You finessed with exhibit "A" on the assumption that "B" was your ace. May I suggest that you consult Mr Bestworth or somebody like him about the letter-heading?'

'But why Mr Bestworth, Canon?'

'He's a printer, isn't he?'

XII

Mrs Fenwick had always approved of Quill. She brought in coffee and sat with him and her husband while she explained how she had come to know Mrs Capper and meet Jack Sherard, the painter. 'But that was more than twenty years ago,' she added.

'The lady and gentleman still seem to be, er, close, Mrs Fenwick.'

'So I have heard, Mr Quill. They have known each other for a long time.'

'They are not,' he coughed, 'exactly married?'

'As I understand it, they are not married at all. I believe this was proposed in the early days of their acquaintance. But Mrs Capper's previous marriage had not been an altogether happy experience for her. In addition, both she and Mr Sherard were beginning to do well in their own professions. Each decided, perhaps,' and she smiled at her husband, 'that professional advancement was more important—and perhaps easier to attain—than success in marriage.'

Quill remained silent: this was not a police concern. But after Mrs Fenwick had left them he did ask the Canon whether he had also known Sherard in those days.

'I knew him only very slightly. I haven't seen him or his work since. I hope to get to his exhibition before it closes. That might give me some idea of what he has become.'

Quill again remained silent, wondering whether a policeman ought to be able to read the character of a man's life and times from paintings exhibited in a gallery. He shrugged. He was beginning to hope that artists and their works could be eliminated from his enquiry.

'This story, sir, of Sherard and his cousin crawling with other village children under the grating of the church floor—I can't see this as more than a coincidence of scene with Pringle's death. I need to simplify basic facts, sir, as things are now, not to complicate them.'

'That makes sense, Quill, I should have thought. But how can I help you? If the persons involved in this death had been looking for some object they thought to have been hidden in the church, it would have been an obvious preliminary to take up a length of floor-grating.'

'The grating was, in fact, the weapon, sir.'

'Very cumbersome, surely?'

'Everything seems to point to spur-of-the-moment decisions or senseless panic. The body was then needlessly wedged under the seat of a pew.'

'Remorse, Quill, or panic? Get it out of sight at once and then do a bunk, leaving the chancel door open, even though everyone knew it was permanently kept shut?'

'You mean by "remorse", getting a body out of sight? Wouldn't a killer push the body under a seat to prevent it from being seen by someone casually peering through a window, sir?'

'And who in all these deserted eyots and marshes would casually peer through a church window, Quill?

We climbed on the graves, on the stones worn with rains,
And we gazed up the aisle through the small leaded panes?

I beg your pardon. You were saying?'

'It would have been a natural instinct to get the body out of sight somehow, sir. The pew-seat would have been the nearest cover.'

96

'So it would.'

'I agree that Pringle and his killer were probably looking for something; and I now think it may have been the old picture that Mr Poleyn remembers seeing there. It may have been there all this time behind those Commandments panels.'

'Quite possible, Quill.'

'Mr Poleyn remembers it on that wall; Sherard remembers it there; Pringle may also have remembered it and have been looking for it.'

'Certainly possible.'

'If then we say, as perhaps we should, that Pringle was in the church-building a day or so before his cousin reached Saint Sebastian, Pringle may either have wanted to ensure that the picture which they both remembered would still be there for them both to see—or that it should have been removed.'

'Possible; but an unsupported conjecture, Quill.'

'It's the art aspect, sir, that keeps on suggesting a connection with Mr Sherard.'

'It's an unusual coincidence.'

'I wish I could break these coincidences, and that's a fact. The Art World, or whatever, is not something we're equipped to understand at Stourminster, Mr Fenwick. That is why I hoped that you and your good lady might give us a tip or two before we are compelled to hand the whole thing over to London. You see, sir, it's not only this valuable Madonna and Child, if that's the right description—a straightforward sort of subject for a church, no doubt, although the colouring in parts seems to have been a bit, er, unexpected, for the Stour Siblings . . .'

'Certainly, Quill.'

'But then the local vicar—again at your suggestion, sir, and we're grateful. Well, as you know, he came and told us,' and his voice rose slightly, 'about another wretched picture of two gardening ladies that he was asked to take care of. Well, it now seems that you think,' and he looked almost reproachfully at Frank Fenwick, 'that this might be even more valuable. That makes two very pricey pictures, that we round here had no idea existed—and they've both vanished.'

'Yes, Quill. And Mr Sherard himself is a fairly pricey painter whose existence was unknown to you until now . . . ?'

'Exactly, sir. He turns up so pat, you see.'

'I am sure that the vicar of Saint Sebastian now wishes that such a rare bird had not fluttered the parish dovecotes.'

'May I ask, sir, how well you know Mr Chew?'

'Not very well. He is in my deanery, of course, and a colleague. Since you are a policeman on duty, I cannot expect you to treat our conversation as confidential: you might have questions that I, as a clergyman, would not answer. That being understood, let me say that I think I under-estimated Mr Chew. I should explain that we were both relying on Mr Poleyn for expert help. I was perhaps unduly disappointed that Mr Poleyn could not join us at the church to help us with our report. I suppose that I took it for granted that Mr Chew would not have informed himself beforehand of the problems we should have to face.'

'Not one, perhaps, to do his homework?'

'Shall I say that he might have done it had he known that there was any homework that needed doing?'

'The sort of gentleman who believes in crossing his bridges when he comes to them?'

'Yes, and as it happens I was very glad to have Mr Chew with me when faced with the horrible situation of finding a decomposing human body in a shut-up church. Mr Chew behaved with coolness and common sense. There was, of course, nothing we could do except report the matter at once: he volunteered to telephone from the village shop while I kept watch outside the chancel door. He returned very promptly and we then waited together until relieved by the local bobbies. And very glad to get away we both were! He didn't say a word on the way home, but I was nevertheless very glad of his company. Chattering would have been intolerable. My own company, worse.'

'Thank you, sir. That fits in with my own idea of the gentleman. Good in a tight spot, as they say, but perhaps not much of a one to plan a complicated manœuvre. He would not be a great reader, sir?'

'Well, Quill, he is a clerk in holy orders, and you must not forget it. But I would judge his habit of mind to be innocently pragmatic rather than contemplative. It is a lonely life that he and his wife lead in their two parishes, and we must not forget that either. Under similar circumstances some clergymen have tended to become a little eccentric. Mr Chew strikes me as sane. Does this answer your question?'

'Very clearly, sir, and thank you. Could I ask whether a gentleman like this would be likely to know the value of pictures or works of art he might come across by accident?'

'Who shall say, Quill? But I understand your question. Let us leave generalities. When I last spoke with Mr Chew I got the impression that he had been most unfairly involved in the custody of a work of art he was quite unqualified to appreciate. He did not tell me exactly what had happened. I did not ask: he was in obvious distress. I thought that you ought to know about it.'

'He must have come to me almost at once.'

'That may have needed considerable guts. I hope I gave him the right advice?'

'Yes, sir, it may help us a lot.'

'I was thinking that you might help *him*, Chief Superintendent. Since we have so far dealt with what Chaucer might call the Prologue to the Parson's Tale, may I hear the Tale itself?'

* * *

'Do you know Mrs Chew, sir?'

Frank Fenwick laughed. 'It seems that this is one of those parson's tales that never gets to the point. No, I do not know the lady. But I am told she has a frugal mind.'

'Like Mrs Gilpin, sir?'

'Yes. I wouldn't push the comparison. My wife, who meets Mrs Chew on women's organisations in the diocese, thinks of her as a compulsive putter-by of anything that-might-come-in-useful. This is a natural and often admirable habit in parson's wives who live in remote country vicarages. But some of these cult-objects might puzzle an inexperienced anthropologist.'

'Perished elastic? Battered brass door-knobs?'

'You touch it off nicely: stove-in water butts, warped and stringless tennis rackets, irreparable earthenware, such things as one might call mute inglorious millstones.'

'Not all rural districts will arrange to have junk collected . . .'

'Quite right, Quill, and the vicarage is not, I am glad to say, a household either to set or follow the bad example of littering verges with pathetic domestic debris. There are the tales, of course,' he sighed, 'of seemingly worthless objects kept long enough to prove of great price.'

The Chief Superintendent looked suddenly alert. 'Do you think that Mrs Chew might have traded-in something of the kind to a travelling . . . ?'

'Really, Quill, I have no means of knowing. I ought not to answer such a question. What the rural dean said is not evidence, eh? Am I now to be entrusted with your tale?'

'Yes, sir, I'm sorry. When the reverend gentleman came to see me he was in great distress lest he should have unintentionally broken faith with his late parishioner.'

'That was my impression.'

'Yes, sir. What seemed to make it worse was the fear lest his lady wife had been unintentionally responsible for his lapse.'

'Does it concern the possible loss of a picture?'

'Yes, sir, by this French painter Vuillard.'

Frank Fenwick groaned. 'He showed you Mr Sherard's latest letter?'

'Exactly, sir, the late Pringle must have wanted to prevent his cousin from seeing this Vuillard picture.'

'Do we know why?'

'Not yet.'

'Well, he didn't succeed. Quite the opposite. I am sure that Mr Chew would not have shown it had he been asked not to. But he might, I think, have declined to accept care of it on such furtive conditions. Had Pringle, before his cousin's arrival, just been keeping the picture in Saint Sebastian School-house?'

'So I presume, sir. The picture must have been the only thing there that he didn't want his cousin to see: he had gone out of his way to press him to come and stay. His cousin would have recognised it all right, as we know from this last letter. He spotted it at once as "a painting by Vuillard that I had previously seen".'

'Well, as I have said, Mr Chew cannot be blamed for showing it to Sherard.'

'Certainly not, sir. When Pringle went missing, the vicar would naturally want to be relieved of the custody of what he regarded as rubbish.'

'Which was worth?'

'Ah, sir, as soon as Mr Chew mentioned your own guess

I decided to telephone our advisers in London. They confirm that it could be worth a very great deal of money. I can well understand the shrewd and careful Mr Sherard, as soon as he had made sure of his position as heir, writing to the poor vicar to ask if the picture was still in "safe-keeping".'

'And was it?' His voice had sharpened a little.

'I naturally asked the same question, sir. At first the reverend gentleman could only repeat, "My wife and I, officer, keep on asking ourselves where this wretched daub can have got to." I think he was half-convinced that his wife had sold it as junk.'

XIII

'Well, you see, sir, there really was junk in those vicarage attics: a smashed rocking horse; a baby's bath; fire-guards, photograph albums—that sort of thing. They had been there for years. When *I* was shown the place it was empty except for one or two dead bats. The rest—and Mrs Chew had a carbon copy of a roughly-pencilled list—had been sold to a travelling scrap dealer.'

'Are there such out there?'

'You know the sort, sir, "any old iron—rags, rags, rags? Morning lady, twenty new pence the lot? Make it thirty for you, lady. I seen that ole iron veranda out the back. Say what, I'll come tomorrow and shift that to oblige. Jest fer today I've got the little ole van outside. Give you a quid fer the gates?" '

'It sounds to me, Quill, like the patter of our old friend, Charley Gotobed.'*

'Well, sir, and that's who it was! Rather far from his base, I should have thought. He must be reduced to scraping the bottom of the barrel to be as far out as the Siblings, um?'

'An engaging rogue, as I remember.'

'No doubt about it, sir. He could talk the tail off a haddock and leave it feeling grateful. It seems that he "happened along" to the vicarage sometime when Mr Chew was out on parish business. Mrs Chew thought it—as no doubt Charley

Worse Than Death.

intended—an excellent chance to clear her attics. Charley took one look and offered to take the lot cash down.'

'Picture included? There, somewhat improbably, seems to have been a list.'

'Well, sir, this is what all the fuss has been about. Mr Chew says the picture was *not* included. It was the first thing he had asked his wife. Mrs Chew had told Charley Gotobed that everything in the attics could be taken "but not the picture because that doesn't belong to us". Moreover the picture was not included on the list which he engagingly scribbled out and gave the lady, with whatever new pence had been agreed. She left him to bring his purchases down the stairs . . .'

'Yes, so far this makes sense.'

'But I suppose that when Mr Chew got home and heard the tale, sir, there was nothing left in the attics but dust and dead bats.'

'As you "suppose"? '

'He was a bit vague, sir. Vague about his wife's part in the transaction. Even though the picture was not on the bill of sale he didn't want to suggest that his wife had let it go.'

'If you are wondering, Quill, whether you can accept that as a strictly truthful account, may I say that I am sure that Mr Chew would not try to mislead you on such an essential matter. If he hoped that you could help him to recover this valuable article he would fully realise the different implications, if it had or had not been included in a *bona fide* sale. He was, in fact, assuring you that it had *not* been included, and was accepting his wife's word for it. He may have been angry with her for not having watched her cast-offs being loaded.'

'She had returned to her interrupted domestic chores, sir; but she had apparently "looked into the back of the van" before it left, and had noticed nothing amiss.'

'She means that she had seen no picture in the van?'

Mr Quill did not answer directly. 'I must say,' he said, 'we should have liked to have known a little more how we stood, if we were going to question Charley Gotobed, of all slippery customers, about the rights and wrongs of his transactions.'

Frank Fenwick felt that a climax was being held back and accordingly waited for the drama of the tale to be developed as Mr Quill wished. 'This Charley,' said Quill with evident relish, 'we had no difficulty in picking him up. As soon as the vicar had left, I telephoned the divisions. Stourport told me that they were at that moment having a friendly little chat with Charley down at Renters Hard. There was nothing in the van, but Charley had been spinning quite a tale and they thought I would like to hear it. They would ask him to wait for me. Apparently there had been a bit of a mix-up on the quays with some visiting firemen.'

Frank Fenwick started to laugh. ' "Visiting firemen", Quill? You're pulling my leg!'

'No, sir, but it's rather a good story. It involves young Mr Jimmy Bestworth and one of his girl friends.'

'Oh, has a Bestworth sprig been getting into hot water?'

'Cold water, actually: mucking about in boats. They were in a dinghy.'

'A ship-wreck, Quill?

> The boat has left a stormy land,
> A stormy sea before her—?'

'Nothing like that, sir,' said the Chief Superintendent, enjoying himself, 'you have forgotten the firemen.'

'Ah, to be sure, so I had.'

*　　*　　*

'Charley happened to be there and saw the whole thing. He had this Mrs Janice Tyler with him in his van at the time.'

Mr Fenwick groaned. 'And the picture as well?'

'Not at that moment, sir.'

'I can understand that Mrs Tyler might, perhaps, have been enough,' said Fenwick.

'Janice Tyler was indirectly to blame for this odd event, sir.'

'She often is, so I hear from Mr Chew. He says that she is a frequent cause of stumbling in others.'

'There was stumbling, all right. She and Charley Gotobed were down by the water-front in his van, "minding their own business". There happened to be a squad—if that's the word —of recruit firemen on the quay. They were being put through their hose-drill, or something. Janice had decided to lean out of the back of the van to watch. It seems that she knew one of the recruits and gave him a coo-ee. He at once began to overdo things, springing about a bit too sharp and so on, until he was told to look to his front, pay attention, wa-ait for it, and so on . . .'

'It seems to come back to me, Quill.'

'Yes, sir. Well I don't know any fire drill these days; and I wasn't there to see what happened.'

'There is always a right way and a wrong way. Something in your tone tells me that on this occasion it went the wrong way.'

'Indeed, sir.' The Chief Superintendent had already begun to laugh once more. 'It was a beautiful day, if you can imagine the scene. An early September Saturday. There were girls in fluttery light dresses; the sun was shining; the water in the bay was sparkling; a lot of skiffs were darting about the moorings; this come-hither and half-clad Janice Tyler was hanging out of her van; the awkward squad, every man-jack of them blushing, was inattentively hefting the hose. You get the scene? Janice's ex boy-friend—if any boy-friend of hers can ever become an ex—well sir, this oaf was at the hydrant-end of the exercise.'

Mr Fenwick again groaned and lightly covered his eyes.

'Eager to impress Janice, no doubt,' went on Mr Quill, 'and not keeping a proper eye on the drill, the silly fellow smartly turned on the hydrant . . .'

'My heavens!'

'Yes, sir. The hose, of course, sprang to life; one of the squad was off balance; the chap with the nozzle found the thing threshing about in his grip; there was a yell from an approaching dinghy, and young Jimmy Bestworth, standing with a boat hook, was caught full in the chest by a terrific force of water.'

'What happened to the poor chap, Quill?'

'You may well ask, sir,' he said, still laughing. 'Master James was nearly gone for a burton; but as good luck would have it, he went down inboard across the thwarts, base over apex, if I may so put it. And all this amid gales of laughter from the assembled bystanders.'

'Keystone Cops, indeed!'

'Yes, but this wasn't the end of the matter. The nozzle by now had been wrestled skywards: what goes up must come down. The glittering arc, traversing the water-front, now approached the dinghy from behind, where the girl-friend, all unknowing and in a thin white frock, had abandoned the tiller to stand and cry for help. On shore someone had rushed to the hydrant so that the soaring jet of water suddenly shortened on the craft. Screams of warning could be heard on all sides, only to be silenced as the cascade in its dying fall overtook and utterly drenched the luckless girl.'

*　　*　　*

'Well, Mr Quill,' said Charley Gotobed delightedly, 'that's my story, same's I give the Super here. And that he'd not deny. You put that tale round, naming no names, at one o' your police smokers, you'll have 'em all rolling in the aisles.

Reckon those clumsy bastards aint done no real damage. Not money-damage, that is. Young gen'lmn winded isself. Young 'ooman found herself wearing a see-through dress unexpected-like . . .'

'Pore lil thing!' said Janice Tyler virtuously, 'right soaked. Thin cotton 'n all.'

'Ar!' said Charley. 'Not proper decent, mate!'

'Come, Mr Gotobed, we were interested in another matter.'

'Wot I done now, then?'

'Do you remember when you were last in Saint Osyth Sibling?'

'Saint O's, mister? Today, ennit, Jan?'

'Nigh on dinner time, Charley.' She giggled.

'Ar. Happen us met, like.'

'Back end o' reverend's pightle . . .'

'Pightle? That's a small piece of field, isn't it Mrs Tyler. Part of the vicarage glebe?'

'Dunno, mister. Coleman plough them at this time o' day. Stubble,' she again giggled, 'bin barley. Wants draining bad, do that'll flood.'

'May I ask why you were in Mr Coleman's pightle, Mr Gotobed?'

'Wasn't doing nothun, then, was I, Jan?' He grinned.

'Nothun, Charley. Happen us met, like.'

'Jan was setting there when I come along.'

Quill was reminded of an absurd jingle about somebody's aged uncle Arley, sitting in a field of barley.

'Arter that,' said Charley Gotobed, 'us druv around, in our carriage, mister. Nice day fer the sea-side! Us took it slow through Stourport, 'cos of the cops,' and he bowed to the local Superintendent, who remained expressionless. 'Well, mister, we wos soon out to Renters Hard. Lot going on, believe you me. Talk of Fred Carno's army! Coo! Fire-drill, ennit? Cor! Them lot must've got fireworks on the brain!'

'Now, me lad,' said the local Superintendent, 'Mr Quill, here, has heard all that. He was asking you about Saint Osyth, wasn't he?'

'Sorry, guv,' said Charley, not looking at all put out, 'wot can I tell you about Saint O's? Did'n do no biz there today. Personal, like I said. Jest me an this young lady, seeing it were Sat'day art'noon.'

'You did some business at Saint Osyth a day or two earlier?'

'Las' week, mister. I were able t'oblige the vicar's lady. Took'n a load of oddments off'n her hands. Name o' Chew, ennit?'

'Was the vicar at home?'

'Did'n see the reverend. Did'n have that pleasure. Good ole bloke, so's I hear. No fuss 'bout the missus neether. Made her an offer fer the lot. She take it!'

'The lot? Where were these goods, Mr Gotobed?'

'Up under the roof, mister. Attics, ennit? Proper muddle up there, too. Rare pickle, most on it. There wos parts of a lil ole sofa not too far gawn. Lil kiddy's horse on rockers, piebald wi' the tail tore out. Look, gents, I got a list same's I give the lady.' He produced a book with sheets interleaved for carbon paper. The latest entry concerned the transaction at the vicarage. The Chief Superintendent glanced at it: he had no reason to suppose that the under-copy differed from the top as mentioned by Mr Chew.

'The vicar tells me, Mr Gotobed, that there was a picture among the goods shown to you. There is no mention of it here.'

'In course not, sir! Oh no, sir! Mrs Chew, she did'n want to part wi' that picture. Def'nite. Wasn't hers, she say.'

'You didn't include it in your offer?'

' 'Sright.'

'Or take it with you?'

'In course not, sir. 'Twern't bought, see?'

'Can you say what it was like?'

'Not reely. It were half come off a bit of old Essex board. One corner curled up, like. There was not even no frame to un. Picture like that's useless, ennit? Leastwise tis to the like o' me, gents.'

'You see, Mr Gotobed, the picture's not there any longer.'

Charley made big eyes at the two policemen and said, 'Well I never!' But the Chief Superintendent did not think Charley seemed flabbergasted.

He said, 'Are you sure that you left the picture in that attic?'

'In course, mister. Roll o' stuff it were. Might a made a sun-blind but weren't no use to me. Tell you somep'n. That roll-up so easy, I reckon that'd bin rolled-up afore.'

*   *   *

'Ah, come in, Mr Quill,' said Mr Chew. 'Kind of you to call. Come in! Martha, my dear, Mr Quill has called again about that wretched picture. You will join us in a cup of tea, I hope, Chief Superintendent?'

Quill thanked the vicar but explained that he was anxious to make a further search of the attic as soon as might be convenient. Mr and Mrs Chew looked anxiously up the gloomy staircase.

The stair, with balustrade of varnished pine, rose to a half-landing where a sash-window was darkened by Wellingtonias.

'Were you able, Mr Quill,' said the lady, 'to track down that travelling, er, dealer?'

'Yes, madam. The name, as you may remember, is

Gotobed. No fixed address. The family moves about in caravans doing odd jobs.'

'He was not an altogether trustworthy character, I suspect,' said Mrs Chew. 'But . . .'

'We like to keep an eye on him, madam, in case . . . Nothing serious, you know.'

'I'm glad of that, Mr Quill. As a matter of fact, I rather liked him.'

'Indeed, he is what you might call an engaging rogue, madam.'

'A snapper up, no doubt,' said her husband predictably, 'of, er, unconsidered trifles. "Unconsidered"? Um. Mrs Chew made it quite clear that the picture was not for sale. Definitely not to be included with the other, er, items of . . .'

'He certainly understood that, sir.'

'Ah!' she said, breathing a little heavily. 'Not on his list, what's more.'

'For what that's worth,' said her husband (Quill thought) a little unkindly.

They had reached the half-landing and paused. From here, through dark branches, they could glimpse the road. There was a thumping as a lorry, loaded with gravel, shot past. It was closely followed by another, and then by a third. The heavy plate glass of the window rattled and shook.

'It does the property no sort of good,' said the vicar, shaking his head. 'I have asked the men to drive slowly through the village. But they are on piece-work, you know. Can't blame them, I suppose. Their masters are in Stourminster?'

'Further afield than that, sir. Big organisation. "Faceless" is the word, I think.'

'Well, it's most un-*four*-chinnit.'

It was lighter in the attics, and from the window the surrounding view was opened up. 'Is that the pightle, sir?' asked Quill.

' "Pightle?" My goodness, you do know your district! Interesting old word. Actually the field you're looking at is known as "Balklands". The "Pightle" is the one beyond with the mound of field-drains just inside the gate. It's all part of my glebe, but the good Mr Coleman of Fullers Farm cultivates it now . . . "Pightle", "Balklands", "Hither Whisticks". It's sad that the old names are now so seldom used.'

'The picture, Martin!' said Mrs Chew.

'Certainly, my dear. You wished to inspect our depleted lumber-room, Chief Superintendent . . . ?'

Quill looked about him. By now even the dead bats had been removed. The place had been swept. It seemed entirely empty apart from themselves. There were sliding panels, however, along one side of the room where the ceiling slope came down to the floor.

Quill hesitated.

'I had a talk with this Gotobed character, Mr Chew. He says, sir, that he did not take your picture. I'm not sure that I believe him. But he does admit that he took it off the sheet of Essex board that it was pinned to. Safer, he said. He also admits that he took the bit of board for the inside of a chicken-run that he knew of. Um.'

'Do you suppose the board could ever have been considered an essential part of the picture, Chief Superintendent?'

'I don't think so, Mr Chew. The canvas had just been temporarily tacked to it, I understand?'

'That is so. That is so. Undoubtedly.'

'Well, this slippery customer asserts that it was no part of the work in question. He says it was not even like a frame, etc., etc. Otherwise, ahem, he wouldn't have dreamed of taking it. And so on. In my opinion, sir, he thought the board it was pinned to would be more useful than the picture.'

'Yes, Superintendent. That does not surprise. It is not far off my own original valuation. However,' and he brightened, 'if Mr Sherard waives claim to the cardboard, I suppose I should now be able to return his other hereditament?'

Quill did not at first reply to the vicar. Then he said, 'Gotobed maintains that the canvas rolled itself up as he untacked it. He said that it must have been previously rolled-up for a long time.'

' "Rolled"?' The vicar looked doubtful. 'Would that do a picture any harm?'

'I don't know, sir. It's a thing experts would know, I don't doubt. But the point is, sir, that Gotobed says he never took it. Left it here, in fact!'

'*Here*, Mr Quill? Martha, was there ever anything rolled-up?'

'I am quite sure there wasn't, Martin. I would have told you so.'

'I was wondering, sir, whether we could see into those cupboards in the skirting?'

'Of course, Quill! Of course!'

They searched all the recesses but nothing did they find.
'Most un-*four*-chinnit!' said Mr Chew.

XIV

'I WAS THINKING, my dear,' said Frank Fenwick at breakfast on Monday, his usual day off from work, 'we ought, perhaps, to look in on this exhibition of Sherard's. I can't get up to London for the Private View tomorrow; but in any case it's his pictures I want to see, not half the members of the London Group. What about Monday of next week?'

'Well, Frank, you won't get into the Whitechapel Gallery on a Monday: it will be shut, shut, shut. Open on Sundays instead.'

'That's a fat lot of use to me! Perhaps next week I could manage a Tuesday? Would that be possible for you, my dear?'

'Oh, I think so. Most of those who have had cards will have been to the show by then and we could look round in comfort. I should certainly like to see what he has been up to recently. If we went up in the morning we could have a sandwich afterwards at that splendid kosher place a few doors away. Is there anything else you might want to do in London?'

'I don't think so. There is nothing on at Lords: it will all be under dust sheets. What is the story of this art gallery in Whitechapel?'

'It started, I think, at the beginning of this century. It's a "charitable institution", founded to organise a succession of free exhibitions in that neighbourhood. There has never been a permanent collection. Recent directors have been putting on *avant-garde* shows, following the lead of the Tate, perhaps? Or even setting the pace for young British and American artists!'

'And what do the native East-Enders think about it?'

'I don't know, Frank. It has a fairly close following from the staff and students of London art schools. I should have thought that Jack Sherard might be a bit out of line from their recent policy: he is too old to be given a coming-out ball and not quite grand enough to be treated as the grand old man of the moderns. The young might even find him somewhat *déja-vu.*'

'How very sad for the poor fellow: however, it's not only the young that he will have to out-face. Quill and Glover of our C.I.D. are watching his every move.'

'Oh, Frank!' she said. 'Can he be seriously implicated in this beastly business at Saint Seb?'

'I can't make it out, Penelope. They seem to think so. I don't; but he's in some sort of a fix.'

'Can *we* do anything?'

'I don't want Mr Quill to make a mistake.'

'Are you concerned for Mr Quill or for Mr Sherard?'

'I admit I was really thinking of the police. They have a *prima facie* reason for watching Sherard. But premature action would be a mistake.'

'Do you mean that it might lead to a miscarriage of justice, Frank? How horrible!'

'It would be very terrible, Penelope. But I wasn't thinking of that; and it would be the last thing that Mr Quill would want to happen.'

'Oh!' she said, rather crossly, 'were you thinking the police "mistake" might alert Jack Sherard? Or that they might technically mishandle their evidence, and let him off the hook? Well, really! Wouldn't that be pretty nauseating for poor Sherard as well as for the C.I.D.? They at least are supposed to have plenty of practice at weaving spider's webs.'

'I like the Chief Superintendent, my dear: I just would not want him to move too quickly in this matter, for everyone's sakes. Not that I think he will: he is sensible and very fair. Of course it would be distressing for Mr Sherard to have quite undeserved accusations made against him. The police are fully aware of this, as your father would tell you.'

'Of course, Frank. I'm sorry. I didn't want to quarrel.'

(Penelope's father, Colonel Grant, had, until his recent retirement, been Chief Constable of the County.* His son-in-law's occasional association however with the Stour-minster C.I.D. was, as the prefatory disclaimers in detective novels say, 'fortuitous' and had had no connection with the colonel's one-time official position.)

'I really can't yet make out what is happening, Penelope. I think I only set eyes on Mr Sherard once, and that was years ago when we met him with Meg Capper at Bertorelli's restaurant.'

'My dear Frank it must be fifteen to twenty years since we last dined at Berts. I don't know Mr Sherard any better than you do. I only know that he's still on visiting terms with Meg. Not that I've seen *her* for ages. I suppose we've lost touch. What am I to say if I should run into her again?'

'About her boy friend having been down here recently? Well, he never got in touch with us: we know nothing about what he was up to. Nor do the police, except what he himself may have told them—and that's no concern of yours. As for Meg herself, if the occasion should arise, I am sure you will know how to take things on with her from where you both left off. I remember liking her. You told me that she never remarried. Does Master Sherard reckon to have set up house with her?'

'I don't think so, Frank. She has her work and always

Death of a Dissenter.

116

intended to keep herself unencumbered. Jack Sherard has his and prefers to live in his own studio. Latterly he has become somewhat of a displaced person. She may put him up in transit: I wouldn't know.'

'A convenient arrangement, you might say.'

'She's a splendid woman, Frank. Better than *he* deserves, I might say, from what I have seen of his work or of the man himself: he's almost entirely cerebral; he seems only half alive.'

'Steady on, my dear. One never knows. To quote the Reverend Cornelius Whurr, not, incidentally, my favourite nineteenth-century divine,

> What lasting joys the man attend
> Who has a polish'd female friend!'

*   *   *

The Fenwicks often visited London together on his 'day off'. They had many friends there. He had held the living of a city church, Saint Asaph by the Postern, and in his early cricketing days had frequented the M.C.C. as well as the haunts of his own profession.

They reached the Whitechapel at about eleven-forty-five on the Tuesday morning, a week after the Sherard show had 'opened'. There were not many people in the gallery and it was very quiet. There had been some small drawings in the ante-room. These they intended—but later forgot—to examine on the way out.

Penelope kept up with exhibitions but was seldom at private views, so that she had ceased to be part of the gallery 'scene'. She was known, nevertheless, to some of the older dealers. Both she and Frank had private means. She bought a painting now and then—a personal choice and usually a very good one. Although their values rose she did not try to resell her pictures, to which she remained very attached. Her favourite was a Morandi still-life—which she had acquired as a rare 'escape' from this mysterious painter's workroom.

Frank visited the galleries less often. He shared his wife's interest, but at a remove. She might be said, in the phrase of Delacroix, to 'taste a picture with the eye'. He was as visually alert as his wife, and technically almost as well-informed; but his interest in 'reading' a painting—whether narrative, figurative or abstract—was to find what manner of man had painted it, and by how much the human spirit became enlarged by stretching the boundaries of visual awareness. The really great painters, he observed, stood any normally-accepted art theory on its head, dusted it down, and turned it the right way up again, still looking a little red in the face.

As they came into the main gallery he stopped for a catalogue. This was a voguish affair with foreword and critical apparatus. But there were no picture-titles: just numbers; and these were printed in words rather than in numerals.

An affectation? Well, thought Frank, titles for pictures like these had long been irrelevant—even such old tags as 'composition', 'arrangement', etcetera. And he supposed that any artist, who had been working day after day on nicely calculated less or more for each picture, might feel that a mere numeral would be a too brief-looking identification. Numerals, moreover, were not this particular artist's method of adding here a little and there a little.

Bless me! The catalogue-cover itself, in laminated white card, is further covered by a sheet of loosely attached transparent acetate. This was in three strips. As he closed the catalogue one of these strips fluttered and settled. He noticed that the butted edges of these integuments fell line upon line of the legend displayed in a new Swiss type face. What now?

He keeps whiter-than-white cleaner-than-clean, subliminally suggesting precept upon precept upon precept? How absolute the knave is! Frank turned his attention to the exhibits.

He was again aware of the silence in the room. There were a few young persons whose clothes were sending out small signals of status and conviction. They moved or stood soundlessly before the pictures. A girl wearing regulation jeans and sandals sat apart on a bench, crouched forward, fingers interlaced, elbows on wide-apart knees. Her face was quite without expression.

Daylight from ceiling lanterns fell unemphatically on white screens and white walls. The dark rectangles of the exhibits punctuated the intervals with precision. Frank's eye was carried from accent to accent; and he noted how each spectator seemed dignified by the scale of the surroundings. He now saw his wife, upright and graceful, moving slowly in the distance between silent groups.

The exhibition, he realised, had itself been beautifully 'hung'.

He said as much when he rejoined Penelope. She nodded and they sat on one of the cross-benches facing the largest and darkest of the paintings; it had involutions of black upon black in bands and trickles. 'Careful Mr Sherard,' said Frank, 'summoning gleams of darkness out of inky chaos.'

'Splendidly null, would you say?'

'Not fair, my dear, not quite fair! There is certainly nothing icily regular.' He grinned and they sat on in companionable silence. I'm enjoying this, he thought.

Towards half past twelve a few business men came in and began to look round with quick glances and some shrugs. One or two others, perhaps from further west, were going round more deliberately; but the general sense of quiet remained. People are behaving, he thought, as if in church. He rose once more to look at the pictures.

Penelope's glance followed him with affection. He doesn't look like any one else here, she thought. He was tall, with a craggy face and reddish tufty eyebrows. His closely curling hair was beginning to turn grey over the ears. He was in 'mufti'—a dark flannel suit, soft collar and knitted tie. She was amused to see him accosted by a little round man with horn-rimmed spectacles and the confident air of one whose foot is on his native heath. She settled down to watch an interchange of fane and forum. This took an unexpected turn.

'Morning,' said this individual to Frank Fenwick, making a rapid estimate of the cost, and perhaps of the provenance, of the clothes he wore.

Frank cheerfully inclined his head, giving as it were conversational entry, should this be what the stranger were seeking.

'Make anything of it?' asked the other, eyeing a picture.

'Very little,' said Mr Fenwick.

'No good, then?'

'Oh, I wouldn't say that. I think I know what he was trying to do.'

'What's that, then?'

Mr Fenwick looked at the picture for some time without speaking. The stranger looked at Mr Fenwick. To do so he had to look up; and his spectacles blindly reflected the roof lighting. Frank was slightly disconcerted to find in each lens a shadow of the ceiling ventilators flicking round—an outward and visible sign of an inward and mental computer?

'Do you think, perhaps,' said Frank, 'that each picture is thought of as part of the whole exhibition? Painted specially for this gallery? I think it's a very good *exhibition*.'

'Good, is it?'

'That is my feeling, yes: everyone is very quiet.'

'Yes. Gets them, does he?'

'Or the arrangement does. I feel very satisfied to go on looking at the room as a whole. I don't have to look at the canvases all the time. But when I do, they seem all right: I don't have to worry what they mean or whether there is anything wrong with them. But chiefly I suppose I like being here, and I like being with others who perhaps feel the same.'

'It's the arrangement, then? No good buying one: you'd have to get the lot? There's no price-list that I can see.'

'It's not one of the commercial galleries, is it?'

The stranger shrugged and again turned his spectacles with the revolving reflections upon Frank. 'Are you a friend of this artist, sir?'

Frank shook his head. 'I met him once about twenty years ago.' He made to move on; but the stranger had not finished.

'I was thinking of a place where people want to meet and be quiet,' he said. 'Would these pictures be suitable?'

'Very suitable, I should say. That is my own feeling.'

'Get hold of him, eh, to go round the walls of a big room? Paint the place out?'

'That might not be quite the same thing? I'm afraid I could not give an opinion. Perhaps the gallery director . . . ?'

'Needs thinking over: I'll ask. Morning! Morning!'

'My dear Frank,' said Penelope, coming up behind him a moment later and slipping her arm into his. 'Please tell me: who was that little man?'

He continued to stare at the wall in front. She gently pinched his arm through the sleeve of his jacket.

'I beg your pardon, my dear,' he said. 'I wouldn't know him from Laban; but I like him. I took him to be a good man . . . What about lunch?'

*　　*　　*

When they were in the street Penelope again pressed his arm. 'You know, Frank, this is a real holiday. We might be abroad.'

It was true. They were being not unpleasantly jostled from all sides by the crowd on the wide pavement. And although they heard nothing but English spoken, the feeling of 'abroad' became even stronger as they turned into the place where they were to have their meal.

There was a serving-counter on the left; and against a wall on their right were stools and a ledge at which people were already eating. Ahead was a screen: beyond that waiters were busily serving at tables with snowy white cloths. Everything was brisk and clean; and they were to find that the more crowded it became, the better humoured.

Penelope spoke up at once. 'Boiled beef sandwiches for us, Frank, with mustard. I shall establish a foothold along the wailing wall here while you order. For pity's sake mind how you get into the counter queue or there'll be a riot.'

He blenched slightly but marked a gap, only to be taken firmly in hand, pushed, pulled, spoken to. Thereafter he shuffled forward slowly and was freely included in the conversation on every side. One powerful lady flashed upon him the smile she reserved for prize-winners.

To all this, however, he gave only part of his mind. He realised that he would either have to gauge correctly when to shout his order, or else fail to arrive in time at the point of delivery. If too late he would clog the works: if too soon he might receive and even devour another's portion. He shuddered.

At one moment in the clamour around him he heard a powerful but beautifully modulated contralto loose upon the eddying air the one word 'Pe-*nel*-o-pe'. He could not turn, for his eye was being engaged by the knife-flashing manciple at the end of the service-counter. He put in his order, saw it taken, sliced, slapped, mustarded, served in paper napkins on plates and started in his direction on an exact collision course.

He duly discovered that it had been Meg Capper, no less, who had recognised and claimed his wife. They had provided space for him and were deep in talk. Mrs Capper looked magnificent: dark, dominating, warm and very much in her natural habitat. He realised that he was delighted to see her again.

Her full attention was like a searchlight. 'Frank, my dear, it must be ages and ages! Neither of you has changed an inch. You both look wonderful. How do you manage it? I'm sure I shall advise all actors to take to cricket, and I shall have to run a mothers' union or something. Penelope tells me that you have been next door to see my poor old boy's pictures. Were they all right? He really has tried, over this show. Such a *fantoccini* it's been, with him fiddling about and muttering! I know Penelope won't like his late-period stuff—nonsense darling, it's not your kind of thing! Or mine, really . . . or mine.'

'Frank thinks they were very well hung.'

'Oh, they were, you know. Bless you, Frank! Nowadays, it seems, hanging is all that Jack cares about. I know that nothing is supposed to be for sale at the Whitechapel, but I don't think the old boy would part with any of them separately. It's the ensemble that matters, the ensemble!' She raised her magnificent eyebrows. 'Crazy! Quite, quite absurd. He's been worrying this show round in his head for ages. That's what all the muttering has been about. Ugh!' Her eyes swung heavenward.

'Lovely beef this,' said Penelope, munching.

'Heavenly! I always come here when I'm down this way. Actually I'm rehearsing this afternoon.'

'I thought you were in Webster at Shaftesbury Avenue, Meg.'

'So I am, darling. But for my sins there is a single-performance theatre club thing down here on Sunday evening. Madness! But it gets a wonderful house. Perhaps the best anywhere. Penelope, my sweet, I couldn't bend you to my will and carry you off to this rehearsal? I promise you it wouldn't be all that boring, and you can be as bitchy as you like about the sets: they are not nearly as good as yours used to be.'

While this was going on Frank indicated encouragement to Penelope and his intention of leaving them together for the rest of the afternoon.

When Mrs Capper brought the conversation round once more to the Whitechapel gallery she said, 'Jack's going round like a bear with a sore head at present. He says he thinks he's being followed, or something mad.'

Frank Fenwick, licking a finger tip, thought it not unlikely. 'Did he have any difficulty in finishing his work for the show?' he asked. 'He had to leave his studio, I hear.'

'Yes, he did. It made him most peculiar. His dealer didn't help: kept on reminding him he'd have to go. Then Jack got this entirely unexpected offer of another place where he could get on with his scratching and patching and matching without interruption. Miles from anywhere, I was about to say, but it must have been somewhere near you, Penelope.'

'Saint Sebastian Sibling.'

'Ah, you know it. I went down to see him one day. I know I ought to have looked you up, darling, but I was learning a part. I couldn't have stopped for a moment.'

'How on earth did Jack come to hear of such a place, Meg? It's not the sea coast of Bohemia, like St Ives or Aldburgh.'

'You may well ask! Some man, a complete stranger, as Jack rather implied, called on him in London and virtually forced the loan of this place on him. Not that Jack was in any condition to refuse, with bulldozers almost nudging his doorstep. It was a most convenient offer. Just what the old bore needed to put a stop to his mutterings and putterings.'

'Do you say this was a "complete stranger"?' asked Frank.

'Well, *not*, actually. Jack didn't, or wouldn't tell me at first, the silly old weasel. I wormed it out of him later. It seems to have been some long-lost cousin, a surveyor's clerk or rent-collector. Or perhaps a tallyman from the Gas Board.' She rolled her enormous eyes. 'I don't suppose you remember Jack, Penelope? He's a funny old thing, sweet in many ways; but he's just a teeny bit of a snob. I don't mean that he goes about casting sheep's eyes at coronets. But he wouldn't think kind hearts an improvement on them. Surely this was a kind offer; but he seems to have been a bit ashamed of his country cousin. Not madly keen to bring him round to the stage door . . . Penelope, we really must be shifting, if you still . . .'

They rose. Frank was watching the restaurant-part of the establishment, amused by the expertness of the waiters in getting a quick turn-round of occupants at their tables. One waiter seemed to be signalling to suggest that a place was becoming vacant for Frank and his party. Frank smiled and shook his head. But he noticed that he was also being watched by someone else.

Mrs Capper said, 'Oh Lord, there's that awful little man from the Cornford. He's spotted us. I'm afraid we shan't be able to get off now without a word or two. Do you mind? I'll try not to get you involved. You see, he's by way of being Jack's dealer. He's not too bad, really, I suppose. He's just madly inquisitive. He wormed out of Jack everything known about that cousin of his. Even what the wretch did in the war.'

'Well, Meg, my dear,' said this individual, rubbing his hands and with an eye on Penelope—the two ladies were a distinguished pair—'have you been down to have a second look at Master Jack's pretty pictures?'

'Very well worth it, wouldn't you say?'

'Undoubtedly! Make no mistake! He knows a thing or two, does Jack. A very downy bird. No stopping him.'

'Would anyone wish to?' said Mrs Capper.

He laughed, stretching up and down on his toes. 'Heaven forfend! What an extraordinary suggestion!' He continued to stare at Penelope with unveiled curiosity. That lady looked back calmly during the lengthening pause.

Eventually Mrs Capper said, somewhat vaguely, as if to whomsoever it might concern, 'This is Mr Rowland Mallender of the Cornford Gallery. Rowley, let me introduce Mr Fenwick. Mr Fenwick is a cricketer of credit and renown.'

Mr Mallender examined Frank briefly, and with a hint of disenchantment.

'And now, if you will excuse us, Rowley,' said Mrs Capper briskly, 'Mrs Fenwick and I must go.' She turned to Frank, 'It's been such fun! Do let us soon arrange another meeting. Sweet of you to let me have Penelope for the afternoon.' Frank and Mr Mallender were left together in the crowd.

'Do you play at Lords?' asked Mr Mallender absurdly and perhaps offensively.

'I have played there, yes,' said Frank mildly, 'but Middlesex is not my county.' He moved as if to invite an end to this unpromising conversation. Mr Mallender moved with him.

'I greatly admire Mrs Capper's acting,' said Mr Mallender.

'And I,' said Frank.

They passed together into the street: by now there was no sign of the two ladies.

'I am thinking of taking the Underground,' said Frank.

'Allow me to walk that far,' said Mr Mallender, 'I am going to the gallery.'

'Of course,' said Frank gravely. 'It will be a pleasure.' He shortened his stride, and after twenty paces or so, they stopped.

'I am not greatly interested in cricket,' said Rowland Mallender; and Frank inclined his head condoning such an admission. 'But I saw rather an extraordinary sight the other day. My motor car had been halted overlooking a cricket ground. I was given rather a good view, hanging as it were with grooms and porters on the bridge.' Frank again inclined his head to acknowledge this point of Eng. Lit. 'Just as the traffic got going again, there was a great shout from the ground. I couldn't see a ball; but one of the fieldsmen— if that is what they are called, the brave men who catch hard balls with their bare hands. One of these stalwarts, a terrifying fellow with a black beard and a turban—could that be? He was a black man?—came racing across the ground at a terrific pace towards the spectators. It was a high catch or something. There he went, leaning back, his knees going up and down at a terrific pace, face turned in supplication to the sky. I didn't actually see his enormous hands close over the tiny object, but he clasped them and took an enormous leap. He ploughed on to become lost to view. The din from the ground was prodigious. But then cars were also hooting behind me. I had to tear myself away from this manly sport, crossing as it does the confines of race and creed and colour. Ahem! But you must be getting on your way, sir, and I on mine. A very good afternoon to you.' He turned into the gallery.

Frank Fenwick did not at once enter the adjoining Underground station. He was lost in thought.

XV

'THE PRESS is being remarkably patient, Charles,' said Quill, looking up from the murder file. 'There can't be many persons in a remote countryside like Saint Seb who would beat a respectable resident to death in church—not that any local is all that respectable. Nevertheless we would expect to have found anyone capable of murder sticking out like a wild oat in the wheat.'

'I am told there have been a lot of wild oats in this year's harvest, sir.'

'Yes, I suppose so. Silly of me. I should talk about sore thumbs. The point is that we had rather given up looking among the Saint Sebastianites for suspects. I wonder if we were altogether right? We have been looking for Londoners. Can we really expect to find bowler hats and rolled umbrellas in all that barley?'

The Inspector did not think this a question calling for an answer. Instead, he replied, 'Sergeant Simmons, sir, would like to be kept on watching the picture galleries. He rather thinks he fits-in up there.'

'He may look like a cop among all those wild oats in the Whitechapel Gallery.'

'I think his eye is on that other gallery in Duke Street, sir.'

'The Cornfield Gallery? Must be full of wild oats, Charles.'

'Cornford, sir. Mr Sherard's home ground.'

'Blast Mr Sherard! We're always coming back to him.

Has Simmons any justification for still keeping his eye on that stuffed shirt?'

'I think Simmons's eye may be on a rather pretty girl in the Cornford Gallery, sir. It's all right. I'm keeping my own eye on him. He's not just poodle-faking. He's found out something. Do you remember the printed letterheads, sir, on the two notes purporting to have been written by Sherard to deceased?'

'Our famous exhibits "A" and "B"? Mr Fenwick said that Bestworth, the printer, could tell us something about their typography.'

'Yes, sir. You may remember that in the end we thought it better to ask the Yard. There's a report coming through. But they telephoned the gist of it. It's not conclusive, but it's interesting. Odd thing for the reverend to have spotted.'

'He's not unnoticing, Charles. Must be all that watching for the ball that comes out of the back of the bowler's hand. Well, even we noticed the two different printing types. Perhaps Sherard kept two batches of writing paper and used them indiscriminately?'

'He's rather a discriminating man, wouldn't you say, sir. Very much aware of the latest trends?'

'Certainly.'

'Not likely to go about with one brown shoe lace and one black?'

'Unintentionally, no. Out with it, Charles.'

'Well, sir, he wouldn't write from one batch on a Tuesday and from another the next week without noticing the difference.'

'Come, Charles. He'd certainly know the difference, but would it matter? It wouldn't to me if I was using up old stock. That's not at all like wearing odd shoe laces or going about with one's fly-buttons open. What does the Yard say?'

'Apparently "A" is a new, smart, Continental typeface,

and "B" was probably old-hat when he first ordered it. He could have had that letter paper for years: provincial jobbing-printer's sort of stuff.'

'Perhaps he didn't want to waste his smart new paper on his provincial country cousin: he would not mind scribbling to *him* on a bit of old tat he found at the back of a drawer? Not conclusive. Where does Sergeant Simmons come in?'

'There are two points here. Firstly, Simmons compared the new "A" with the Whitechapel exhibition catalogue: same type face. Sherard seems to have adopted it quite deliberately.'

'May be, may be. The sergeant is a good sergeant, but . . . well, dammit?'

'Quite so, sir. But Simmons was also speaking to the girl at the Cornford Gallery. She's a Miss Ramage, the secretary-assistant. She looked for letters from Sherard in their files and confirmed that he had only just started using the new writing paper, whereas he had been sending them letters on the old-fashioned stuff for years and years.'

'Right, Charles. But this is getting us nowhere unless we ask Sherard when he finally stopped using the stuff. No doubt we should have done this sooner, instead of "finessing", as the Canon said. Well, you or the sergeant had better take it up with Sherard as soon as you have all the jots and tittles and serifs from the Yard. We may yet find that the letter killeth. Where were we before we got on to "p"s and "q"s?'

'You were saying, sir, and I agree, that we should have another look round for possible local suspects.'

'Not among the oicks and yahoos, would you say?'

'I scarcely think so.'

'Are the publicans the sinners?'

'We-ell, there is nothing . . .'

'Either of the parsons?'

'Certainly not, sir!' He seemed scandalised.

'Or their wives?'

'Sir! I don't see how they could possibly come into it. The idea is . . .'

'Absurd, Charles. However, there could be a woman's foot-marks alongside Pringle's. We were looking, were we not, for someone with smallish feet?'

'Yes, we were. It could possibly be a woman wearing low-heeled shoes. This Janice Tyler always seems to be about in a variety of mixed company; and she blurted out that she was outside the church that very night. Master Plumb, who was probably with her, tried to establish that he had been elsewhere.'

'And so he may have been. A little love and good company is all very well but an alibi is better if a man is to be suspected of murder . . . But footprints, Charles. The small ones, I think, are probably a man's; but he might not be the killer. It is a probability that he was, but no more than a probability as yet. The two of them, Pringle and small-foot, might conceivably have been shuffling round the East End on some previous reconnaissance. The actual killer may have been very careful to leave no traces. Or he may have had no occasion to get near the stamping ground in the sanctuary. The two parsons may have unintentionally obliterated any faint marks before they reached the pew where they found the body.'

'That really would leave it wide open, sir,' said the Inspector, glumly. 'At that rate we could be looking for big-booted Plumb, who so anxiously denied being near.'

'Is there the slightest evidence that it was Plumb?'

'None.'

'So before we start looking for fresh suspects we had better eliminate the somebody with smallish feet, who was most probably a man and certainly must have been with Pringle either soon or immediately before his death.'

'Certainly, sir,' said the relieved Inspector.

'And have we any suggestions, apart from footprints, of anyone who may have been footloose that night?'

'Connected or unconnected with the van?'

'Oh, either, Charles. The van may or may not become evidence: the footprints are already.'

'I reckon, sir, there are four locals whose feet might fit. Motive and opportunity unchecked so far. Just four pairs of feet.'

'Let us have them, Charles.'

'Young Jimmy Bestworth, for one.'

'Indeed, was he ashore? I thought he was welcoming the wild north easter over the German foam.'

'Hadn't liked it, sir. It turns out that at the time we want they had been beating up and down off shore. They had put in three or four times at Renters Hard. I could check further.'

'Right. Check Master Bestworth. Next?'

'His girl friend, sir. Very taken with each other at present. She's the one who got soaked in the dinghy.'

'Whither thou goest, I will go, eh? You are thinking of courting couples in the van, perhaps, in spite of what Canon Fenwick told us about the noises of moving drapery. The prints were in church, remember. Did this compliant lass also consort with the not very attractive Pringle?'

'We don't know yet, sir.'

'But will look into it? Splendid, Charles. Who is next, with dainty tripping toe?'

'Janice Tyler?'

'What a rout of maenads and bassarids you are collecting, Charles! Your fourth?'

'Charley Gotobed, sir?'

'My hat! I could believe anything of him or of his where-abouts. Any time. Day or night. Shoes all right?'

'Very neat and small.'

'Um. Footloose, all right. Anything else about him?'

'Plenty, since we started questioning him about the vicar's attics. He seems implicated with other carryings on at Saint Osyth.'

'Such as?'

'There's Janice Tyler, sir.'

'We know about that, don't we? Any other reason for haunting Saint Osyth or Saint Sebastian?'

'There's been some competition with one of the sand lorry drivers over a girl at Saint Seb. The man can't make un-scheduled journeys—at least not easily. Charley can.'

'Easy as kiss your hand! Can you tie him down to Saint Sebastian on the night we are interested in?'

'Not yet. But I don't think he was far off. He has no normal beat nowadays. His motto is *ubique*, if the gunners and sappers will forgive the comparison. Well, have you asked Mrs Tyler where he was? I must say I wish the long-suffering Mr Tyler would keep some sort of a check on her.'

'She's very fond of her husband, I believe.'

'She's a little friend of all the world, Charles. But this Gotobed, save the mark. Do you think we had better pick him up and put him through the wringer?'

'Yes, sir, I do. We found that bit of Essex board the reverend's picture had been nailed to. Charley had flogged it to someone with a chicken house.'

'The board? Did you find the picture too?'

'No, but I think Charley's got it stashed away somewhere.'

* * *

Sergeant Simmons peered disconsolately through the large window of the Cornford Gallery. He did not know whether any of the Biretta metal sculpture had been sold: it had all been taken away. Judith Ramage's desk stood just inside the door with a pile of catalogues on it. Otherwise nothing was to be seen but polished parquet floor and bare walls. He sighed as though the vanished Birettas had been the most desirable objects he had ever known. Gone . . .

He sighed again. But a movement caught his eye at the top of the basement stairs. Judith Ramage was coming up. She paused and waggled her fingers at him. She signalled for him to enter.

When he joined her he found that she was about to bring a collection of framed prints upstairs. He hastened to help, and soon, under her direction, had arranged these along the skirting-board of the front gallery. The two of them changed some of these over with a giggle or disrespectful comment, trying for greater contrast or better congruence.

'What would all these be?' he asked.

'Silk screen prints. Very fetching, very valuable, very *good*.'

'Silk screen, do you say?'

'Photo-prints, actually.'

'Photo? Not originals, then.'

'Original *prints*.' Firmly. 'And not a word otherwise!'

'They are by different artists?'

'Yes, and all signed, I hope you see. It's the Cornford collection. These three—I don't think we'll hang them together—are by your pal Sherard.'

'Printed by his own fair hand?'

'No. Made in Switzerland. He was there at the time. I believe it took him ages and ages to give the O.K. on them.'

'To make sure that the colours were dead right?'

'You're coming on! Can you help with this mighty metal band? You will find that your end fits that slot in the corner. There are one or two more of them to fix if you can bear it. Then we can get the stuff up from the floor before I kick the glass in.'

He was only too pleased to go on lending a hand—the

nearest he could contrive to holding one. The bars eventually made a continuous strip on the walls at shoulder height. The prints were in frames of uniform size with attachments at the back to engage this impoverished dado-rail. Judith, now wearing cotton gloves, hooked the pictures on to the rail, sliding them this way and that to adjust the spacing, and polishing the glass with a duster.

'Finger-prints,' she said, making a face at him. 'If you were a man in blue instead of in those beautiful, far-from-plain-clothes, you would already have frightened away the rude boy who is breathing on my shop-window.'

A youth was, in fact, doing just this, with both palms spread and nose flattened against the glass. Simmons instinctively moved in his direction with heavy tread; but the street urchin merely put his tongue out and then pursed his lips in what was probably a wolf-whistle. When the boy really had gone, Simmons borrowed the duster, stepped on to the pavement and removed the snail's trail from the glass.

'It all looks jolly attractive from out there,' he said proudly as he re-entered the gallery.

He was rewarded with, 'You deserve a coffee, Detective Sergeant Simmons. If you will descend to our augean basement, I will put the kettle on.'

The basement was certainly a thought depressing: overlit with fluorescent tubes and smelling of damp. They leant against picture racks as they drank the coffee. Higher up were shelves containing box-files, arranged, he supposed, in date order rather than alphabetically. There were one or two of these missing. There was a gap in the older files as well. He did not wish his scrutiny to seem too obvious. 'Is this an advertised show?' he asked, and indicated the prints he had helped to hang upstairs.

'Not yet. It's really a stock exhibition we put on between the others. Mr Mallender is in Paris. At least that's where I think he is. I didn't book his flight for him and I don't really know when he's coming back. It's a bit awkward, he's taken the key of his office with him and there are one or two files and things in there I want to get at. He should be bringing the next show of pictures with him. In the meantime,' and she shrugged, 'it isn't all that difficult keeping an eye on those prints upstairs, although I must confess I find them a bit of a bore. That other ghastly girl takes over tomorrow; so it won't be so bad. I might even do a day's shopping.'

'I have to be in court tomorrow,' he said dejectedly.

She said nothing but regarded her elegant feet, wriggling her toes. Then, 'Dear Mr Simmons, do tell me what's in that pompous-looking brief case you've been dragging around. Hand-cuffs? Dark glasses? A false beard?'

'Photographs,' he said.

She blushed, and for some reason that she could not understand said, 'Oh, are they quite horrible?'

He was taken aback at the suggestion. 'Not at all: just various persons we want identified.'

'May I see them or are they all top secret or something?'

When he spread them out she laughed. They looked very sordid under the uncompromising light. 'What a dreary lot! My word, look at this old boy without a collar. He looks like the frog footman before going upstairs to answer the bell. Really, they're too depressing. Hullo! Mr Simmons, I'm ashamed of you! You've been trying to catch me out. I ask you! This one is none other than nice Mr Sherard. What do you think you are up to, slipping him into the pack among all these ghastly spivs and touts? How did you get this candid camera shot? He quite obviously didn't know any photographer was about. It's just like him. As usual he looks as if he had a smell under his nose. Being a bit up-stage, eh?'

'It *is* Mr Sherard, yes. I certainly wasn't trying to trap you. But we have to be careful. Someone else who ought to have spotted this photograph passed it over. Of course, one can easily miss something when there are so many to look at.'

'Well, you goof, why didn't you just show me the one and say, "Does this remind you of anyone?" I would have got it first time.'

He smiled.

'Wait a moment,' she said. 'Hold your horses! I think I must also have seen one of the others before. This chap. It isn't the lavatory attendant at some Gents, or anywhere else where I couldn't possibly be expected to have been? It isn't another of your traps?'

'Certainly not! You *might* have seen this man before. Quite possible. Any idea when or where?'

Her face brightened. 'Yes, I believe so. I've got it! He's a rather dreary little man who used to come to see Mr Mallender about a year ago.'

He was surprised. 'Do you remember his name?'

She shook her head. For a moment the sergeant even ceased to notice how pretty she was. He was becoming decidedly interested. He waited.

Then she said, 'Now I come to think of it, I never knew his name. He used to come in with Mr Mallender and go straight through to the inner office. I think Mr Mallender always saw him out. He never stopped to look at the pictures.'

'All right. Have you ever seen him with anyone else?'

She shook her head. She thought the sergeant was like one of those large, gentle, pale-tea-coloured dogs. He was very sweet when fetching and carrying for her. But he would be 'in court tomorrow': she was not likely, perhaps, to see him again. Why, she wondered, had he turned up so early this morning? To ask these unimportant questions? There were other questions, perhaps, that might not be very nice? Identity parades? She sat up.

'Oh!' she said. 'That rather common-looking man: I think
I once heard Mr Mallender call him "Pringle".'
He looked very pleased.
She put her hand to her mouth, 'Not . . . ?'
His expression did not change. He nodded very slowly.
She turned away from him. 'Oh, no!'

*　　*　　*

Janice Tyler and Charley Gotobed were in a new spot. It
was at the edge of the field called Balklands, by the dark
windings of the Osyth brook—a shallow stream lined on
either bank with ancient oak and thorn. Janice was now
busily picking burs off her post-office trousers. Charley lay
face-down beside her in the long grass. They had not spoken
for some time. A water rat watched on the further bank
before launching himself with a trail of ripples to hug his own
shore.

There was a dried muddy patch of shingle in midstream;
and a streak of sunlight, sifting through the over-arching
trees, lay like the bloom on a fruit where it touched the
water, like a skein of wool where it reached the mud-bank.

Janice made this comparison to Charley but got no
answer. She rolled over, and with the tip of a finger twiddled
a curl on the nape of his neck. He paid no attention. She
shrugged, staring at the surrounding willow-herb, bell-bind
and sow-thistle. The monotonous call of a small bird sounded
from the opposite bank, a muted note with the frequency of a
far-off unanswered telephone.

'Reckon I'll be off then,' said Charley.

'Do you, love?' said she.

'Bloody Osyth!' he said.

'What's up, mate?'

'Should'n never a come!'

'Please yerself, I'm sure!'

138

There was another silence, then he heaved himself up on one elbow and looked at her. 'Perlice bin onter you, then?'

'Me, luv? What I done? Ole Ben come in Hurdlemakers wunst with his helmet. But *he* aint said nothun.'

'Not him, gal. That other two-faced, toffee-nosed bastard. Sar'nt, ennit?'

'Seen him wunst, I reckon. Spoke pleasant, like. He did'n arst me nothun. What's got into you then, Charley, boy? What's the set-out? Reckon you's scared, like! There aint no call fer you to tantalise me. I aint done nothun, and that's no word of a lie. C'morn! You says you's going. What's holding you, then? You and I aint seen no police, not since that lot down Stourport, along o' that lark with the firemen.'

He heaved himself round and away from her. He began plucking grass. His face was like a thundercloud. 'First off, then,' he muttered, 'I reckon you told the tale that you bin with me or seen me in me van down by the church the night the bloke were done in.'

She scrambled to her feet, appalled. 'Oh Charley,' she said, 'was that you, then?'

'No, gal! And you know damn well that weren't! Can't you keep your trap shut fer jest one minnit? Now jest you listen to me. P'raps you'll remember you aint seen me here today, nor last night neether. Not bleeding never! Get it? Well, I'll now be off, mate. Seeing you . . .'

'But Charley . . .'

'You git home separet. Separet. See?'

XVI

'AND HOW DID YOU find Meg?'

'It was delightful seeing her again, Frank, after such a long time. It's years, isn't it? And thank you for leaving us together. I enjoyed the whole outing. As you said, White-chapel is like abroad. I had even almost forgotten how good those boiled beef sandwiches can be. To my mind they were better than all that Sherardery on show in the gallery.'

'Oh come, my dear! The two experiences perhaps are not strictly comparable? What did you and Meg talk about, if it is permissible for me to ask?'

'Theatre mostly. My word, it's changing. She even asked me if I wouldn't design her . . .'

'You would like that, Penelope? Or has the break been too long?'

'Far, far, far too long, Frank! It would be quite out of the question unless I seriously intended to get right back into all that world again. Meg saw it, of course. As a matter of fact we didn't talk much about the old days. She is not really one for the "do you remember?" thing. She lives very much in the present, does Meg.'

'And for the present?'

'What does one mean by living "for" the present? I would not say that Meg had ever been one to throw her bonnet over the windmill. What an absurd expression that is, Frank.'

'Indeed. Not an easy thing to do without a lot of practice,

I should say. It's from the French, isn't it? Perhaps their mills are less upstanding than ours. However, let us not be Quixotic. Are we on the point of asking each other whether Meg and Jack Sherard are living as man and wife? Not, I suppose, that it is any business of ours.'

'I should not think it is a case of *All for Love, or the World Well Lost*. I gather that she is giving him house room in London while he hunts for another studio. It's not a thing he will find easily.'

'Perhaps he's in no hurry to leave her hospitality.'

'Well, I don't know where she would draw the line; but I don't think she would let him loose with his paints in her own flat.'

'Don't you think she really admires his work and puts up with his prissy ways for the sake of his art? Or is it the other way round? Or are they just good friends?'

'I think she admires his work more than I do. It has a restful sort of backcloth quality. She thinks her "poor old boy" has something to say and that he needs to be given peace and quiet to go on saying it.'

'Would she let his peace and quiet interfere with her career?'

'Certainly not! She may live for the moment in some ways; but she's a real pro as far as the theatre is concerned. She has an eye on her future there, all right. Heavens, yes! And who shall blame her?'

'Not I, my love. Not I.' He looked at her apologetically, thinking of her own renunciations.

She smiled. 'Meg is a wonderful actress, Frank. She has a voice like a bell. I should never forgive Jack Sherard if he got in her way.'

'Perhaps what is more important is whether *she* would forgive him . . . ?'

'Well, she seems to have been trying to protect him from

all these policemen who follow him about or turn up unexpectedly to ask questions.'

'How could she protect him, my dear? I hope she has not been telling lies about where he may have been? Or saying that he is too ill to be questioned?'

'She might do that, I suppose.'

'I can't think of any policeman, not even a young and relatively inexperienced one like Simmons, who would fall for that if he thought there was a case against her precious lodger.'

'Is there, for heaven's sake?'

'The police have thought so, from time to time, Penelope.'

'Have they any evidence, Frank?'

'Of a sort. I don't think it as convincing as they do. But Mr Quill is not likely to rush to unjustifiable conclusions. Nor, on the other hand, is he likely to stop trying to make them justifiable.'

'What sort of evidence, Frank, or can't you say?'

'Well, I can't, my dear; except that they are still worrying away at dates and times of poor Mr Pringle's death and of Mr Sherard's first arrival: diaries, appointments, hotel registers. Routine stuff, you might think. All I hope is that Mrs Capper is not so careless of any bonnets she may have thrown over windmills as to invent stories that her "poor old boy" could have been found in her bed on any particular night he needs an alibi for.'

'Oh, Frank, is that likely?'

'Which probability are you questioning, my love?'

'Do we have to go into all this?'

'Certainly not. I am sorry.'

'I mean to say, Frank, I don't suppose she would care a straw, except that she would not deliberately put herself to the bother of having to give evidence.'

'They seem to be a somewhat selfishly attached pair.'

'Frank,' she said, rather abruptly, 'that little man turned up again after Meg's rehearsal.'

'I do beg your pardon, my dear. Such speculations about her are distasteful. Which little man?'

'I was with Meg in her dressing room; and the A.S.M.— an absurdly pretty girl who looked about sixteen years old— most apologetically put her head round the door to ask if Meg would see a Mr Mallender who had "sent in his card". She seemed to enjoy using this expression.'

'I didn't take to Mr Mallender.'

'Nor does Meg. She made a face, and encouraged this child to stay with me and ask how an Assistant Stage Manager could become a stage designer. Meg was back in next to no time, dusting her hands, as it were, of this stage door johnnie, as she called him.'

'What was Mr Mallender up to?'

'Meg assured us that the wretched man just wanted another look at me. She undertook to see me out by a side door. She made an absurdity of it: rolled her eyes, sank her voice, "such men are dangerous"! The little A.S.M. was delighted—a charming child.'

'But seriously, Penelope, what did this chap want? I really do hope that he didn't waylay you. I have a particular reason for asking. Meg is not far off the mark. He might be dangerous.'

'Darling Frank, I didn't see him again, I promise you. I think that all it amounts to, as Meg said, is insatiable curiosity: he wanted to know exactly who we were.'

'I thought as much.'

'Oh, why, Frank?'

'Mr Mallender may have said something to me that he "didn't oughter".'

'Heavens! Did you two have a long talk after Meg and I left that restaurant?'

'Yes. Not very long. I wanted to get rid of him. He couldn't resist baiting the hearties.'

'My poor dear Frank, what on earth? Oh, now I remember: Meg, being very discreet, or intending to be distinctly naughty, introduced you as a cricketer. The poor little man wasn't to know who you are.'

'Just as well.'

'But why? Oh, oh, oh, that explains it!'

'What explains what, my dear?'

'Meg told me that clever-dick Mr Mallender had dashed off to a public library to consult reference books about us.'

'Ah!'

'Well, Frank, he wouldn't have found much about you in *Wisden*,* surely?'

'No, indeed. It presents an uneventful non-career. But you forget, my dear, that even in *Wisden* I am entered as the "Rev. F.". This chap had only to fly to *Crockford*† to find all the rest.'

She began to laugh. 'But my darling, darling Frank, don't be so absurd! What can it matter? You speak as though *Crockford* recorded long spells of criminal detention, a bigamous marriage or two, some fire-raising and fraudulent dealings on the Stock Exchange.'

'Ah, my dear, *Crockford* can be more severe even than that. But you are quite right. Let us hope that it cannot matter to you what he may find.'

**Wisden Cricketers' Almanack.*
†*Crockford's Clerical Directory.*

XVII

'MR QUILL TO SEE YOU, Frank. He hopes you won't mind his coming a little sooner than he said. Remember, you are going to see Mr Chew later. Have the Chews found the beautiful black madonna?'

'No my dear, I don't think this is going to be about the Chews' problems. I am afraid it's *Crockford* coming home to roost. Please ask Mr Quill to come in.' He put his work aside. 'It was kind of you to call, Quill. I hope what I have to tell you will not be a waste of time. Do sit down. You were looking, as I remember, for the person who made an appointment to meet Pringle in or near the church at Saint Sebastian?'

'We were, indeed. We hadn't entirely ruled out a local, sir, although we can't see why any of them should . . .'

'Have you actual evidence pointing elsewhere?'

'Nothing water-tight. But it seems likely that the killing was in some way connected with the art world.'

'Otherwise the coincidences would need explaining?'

'Indeed. I am sure that that is where I ought to be *looking*. Finding is another matter. This Sherard now . . .' he tailed off rather wistfully.

'You thought that Pringle was killed two days before Sherard was actually seen in the village? Could he have been killed later than that? I'm thinking of the medical evidence.'

'He might, but only just. And if he wasn't killed on Tuesday the tenth, what happened to him? No one saw hair or hide of him from then on. It is true that no one looked for him or rapped on the door of his house until Sherard did just that, in full view, on the Thursday. Sherard not only found the place deserted. He later found the living-quarters in considerable disorder, as "though it had been hastily searched, but with nothing to suggest that Pringle had intended to leave".'

'But he *had* intended to leave, Quill, according to your account. He had made a reservation with his former land-lady in Chelsea.'

'What Mr Sherard meant, or perhaps intended us to think he meant, was that Pringle had left the house without apparently taking a suitcase or bag for the journey. After all, Sherard had not been expecting his cousin to leave until after he had arrived himself.'

'We are arguing both ways, Quill: that Pringle expected to leave some time after his cousin's arrival on the Thursday; but we would like him killed after his cousin's surreptitious—and perhaps suppositious—arrival on Tuesday; because a "strange van" is (not at all convincingly) reported to have been seen outside the church that evening. I know, Quill, that you have never relied too much on the certainty that this van belonged to Mr Sherard, but rather on the evidence of his note, which made an appointment for that very "p.m.". But I haven't told you my story, Quill. I think it may be relevant.'

'That's very clear, sir, and quite fair. Before you tell your story, may I now admit that the wretched note may not in fact mean what we had supposed? You were again quite right, sir, to query the letter-head. Remarkable hunch of yours. Excuse me,' and he referred to his note book. 'We've had a report from the Yard full of all sorts of technicality: printer's stuff about "monotype", "founder's size", "Didot", whoever he may be. I won't bother you with it. To cut all this guff short, they say "the type face used on your specimen 'B' might no longer be considered artistic even by small jobbing printers, although there have been a few respectable examples of its use in book work." Um! They say that the name, if you're interested, sir, is "Cochin Bold". Sounds like poultry to me.'

'Oh, is that what it's called?' said Frank, grinning. 'The wretched stuff used to plague me when I was a curate. There was a little printer who used it on programmes for church concerts. I can well understand Mr Sherard no longer thinking it "artistic".'

'Well, sir, I don't mind admitting it, in things artistic we get a bit off course. Lucky we took your advice to call in the experts; what the Yard calls "a typographical opinion". Mr Sherard's most up-to-date Sandby Studios letter-head was done from a type only released four years ago.' He grinned mischievously and read from his note book, ' "It's a hot-metal Univers fount Series 685 5D".'

'Spare me, Quill, whatever other nonsense did I lead you into?'

'You suggested I should go straight to Mr Sherard and stop "finessing".'

'That was a bit of cheek on my part. I'm sorry.'

'No, sir. You were quite correct, sir. It produced results, all right, although not the ones I expected. Sergeant Simmons had been keeping an eye on Mr Sherard and this Mrs Capper in London. He called on them to ask the gentleman if he knew anything about this note he seemed to have written to his cousin the day before his death.'

'And did Mr Sherard wince on aesthetic grounds (as I had done) or like a guilty thing surprised?'

'He waved it away, sir.'

'What?'

'He seemed impatient, the sergeant tells me. He wanted to

know when we were going to recover his valuable picture from the Reverend at Saint Osyth Sibling.'

'Not unreasonably. It will be worth a lot of money. He may even be very fond of Vuillard's work. It probably influenced his own development as a painter.'

'Simmons was able to say that the vicar had put the matter in our hands. Mr Sherard said something rather rude about pictures not being as simple as dog licences. Then the sergeant caught it from Mrs Capper, who told him "he seemed to waste his time asking absolutely trivial questions instead of minding his proper business". Not fair, of course, and I expect she knew it. I don't suppose that Simmons found this the most propitious moment to revert to our precious letter "B". But he's a good lad. He stuck to it.'

'I see you've got it there. May I have another look at it?'

They looked together at the brief message:

(B)
5, Sandby Studios,
London, W6

9 Aug

Yes. Let's liberate it. Be with you tomorrow p.m. Wishing you make the necessary arrangements.

Jack

'And did Mr Sherard wave it away once more?'

'No, sir. Simmons seems to have pacified them both. But there was no talk about printing type or any of that caper. Mr Sherard's actual words were, "It looks like a message from me. Where on earth did you find it, sergeant?"'

'And did Simmons tell him?'

'No, sir. Instead, he asked him if he remembered writing it, to which Mr Sherard replied, "I haven't the foggiest recollection of doing so. Is it important?" When the sergeant pointed out that it had been dated as recently as the ninth of August, Sherard replied,' and Quill smiled at Mr Fenwick, ' "My dear good chap, I don't suppose I've used writing paper like that for ages. Where *did* you dig it up?" '

'And the sergeant told him?'

'No, sir. I suppose the sergeant stalled. He actually asked whether the *message* might not suggest to whom it had been written.'

'A suave sergeant and slow in his approach.'

'The gentleman, sir, seemed genuinely puzzled. But, you see, the sergeant had been keeping his eyes open. He had been looking for anyone likely to have had letters from Mr Sherard and had actually been shown some written on this early writing paper. He now suggested that our exhibit "B" might have something to do with a picture sale.'

'And did this sprat catch a masterpiece?'

'It seems to have given Mrs Capper a brain wave.' He looked at his notes. 'She said, "I know what it was, Jack. Nice old Mr Murgatroyd got your picture back from the man who gave you a stumer cheque." '

'Who was this kind gentleman, or doesn't it matter?'

'It was a dealer who some years ago was backing Mr Sherard. Mrs Capper then went on to say, "I remember, darling, because afterwards you very sweetly gave it to me. And there it still is, over my desk, hanging next to the Dufy." '

The Reverend Frank was heard to mutter something about a 'polish't female friend'.

'The sergeant,' Quill continued, 'thereupon asked permission to look at this picture. He describes it as "a small still-life sort of thing, signed and dated 1961". So the letter wouldn't have been written before then if the lady's story is true.'

Frank said, 'She might be asked when it really was written. But a calendar is rather a parson's sort of thing. If you want Sherard to have written on a Monday so that "tomorrow p.m." can be a Tuesday the tenth of August, as it was *this* year,' and he grinned at Quill, 'the only other year reasonably close would have to be 1965.'

'Yes, sir,' said Quill modestly, 'the sergeant had worked that out for us.'

Mr Fenwick bowed, 'I beg your pardon, Quill. "Elementary", to coin a phrase.'

'Not at all, sir. You are very quick. The sergeant set off on his rounds again, not to find the letter, which, of course, we already had, but to find the correspondence from which it might have been removed.'

Mr Fenwick groaned. 'My dear chap, wasn't that a hopeless quest?'

'No, sir. "Routine" is the word. He's a good lad, is the sergeant; and he was lucky. He didn't have access to the correspondence itself; but he found in a 1965,' and he grinned at Mr Fenwick, 'letter-register at one of the offices, the following entries under "out" and "in" respectively: "5 Aug. Murg.—Sherard. Suggest threaten legal action; 10 Aug. Agree from Sherard." We think that is the note Mrs Capper identified.'

'Well, well, well! What more could you want? Rolled round in earth's diurnal course with dates and notes and years! An almanac-fancier's joy!'

'As you say, sir,' said Quill smugly.

'Does that let poor Mr Sherard gasping off your hook? And was he thereupon told where the purloined letter was found?'

'No sir, the answer to your second question is that Simmons deemed it a matter best left to us at Headquarters.'

'So. Sherard is yet to learn that an innocent note he had written six years ago had been conspicuously stuffed into his dead cousin's pocket. Do I now suspect something even more wicked than murder?'

'Indeed, sir. That note had been planted to incriminate him. It's wicked, all right. It is one of those stupid, unnecessary, far-too-clever touches that the police come to recognise only too well. The bloke must have hugged himself with—what was the phrase?—ah, "an almanac-fancier's joy". He had found something that seemed to fit perfectly into what he was planning. Or it may even have suggested the plan. Either way, he simply could not deprive himself of the joy of using it. But it's going to trip him up. He's going to fall smack on his smug, clever face. But I'm so sorry. I still haven't let you tell me what I specially came to hear.'

* * *

'It will be an anticlimax after all this excitement, Quill. But if you still want an intruder from the art-world who may have been near Saint Sebastian on the tenth of August, I can suggest one.'

'I should be grateful.'

Frank told of his visit to the Whitechapel Gallery and of the subsequent encounter with Mallender. 'You see, Quill, I was wearing what you might call plain clothes and had been briefly introduced as a "cricketer" and not as a parson. When the ladies withdrew I think Mr Mallender may have felt that he had been palmed off with a buffoon of sorts when he had hoped for an interesting session with what my father would have called a "pair of absolute stunners".'

Quill wondered whether anyone would ever mistake the reverend gentleman, however dressed, as any kind of buffoon; but he said nothing, and Frank continued. 'There we both were, myself rather tall and he rather short, trying to make conversation while being jostled by the busy burghers of Whitechapel.'

Quill said, 'I know the place. It's near Aldgate East Underground Station.'

'The station was just in sight. I said I was making for it. He then, for no reason that I could discern, began to subject me to some rather heavy-handed banter.'

'Sir?' said Quill, scandalised.

'He may be the sort who thinks any middle-aged sportsman fair game. Many of them are. Be that as it may, he detained me in Whitechapel High Street with a pointless *histoire* of a cricket match that he had seen for a brief moment while he had been held up in a traffic jam. His car had been on a bridge overlooking the ground.'

Quill, perhaps thinking that if the anecdote was pointless he did not wish to hear it, interjected rather brusquely, 'We know about Mr Mallender, sir. He's the director of the Cornford Gallery.'

'So I was told when we were introduced. I did not think it important at that time.'

'I mention it, sir, because it was at that gallery Simmons was able to identify Mr Sherard's letter. Mr Sherard's old friend, Mr Murgatroyd, used to be the managing director. It was all in the letter registry. Simmons hadn't access to the file itself, which happened to be locked in Mr Mallender's own office. We think that Mallender had meanwhile taken the incriminating note out of the file.'

'How very frightening,' said Frank Fenwick sharply. 'I had better finish my story so that you will know what to do. His pointless cricket anecdote was a very circumstantial account of a particular incident involving a spectacular catch. There are many roads that overlook cricket grounds in this country; but traffic jams on the Parks Road flyover certainly give motorists a free view at Stourminster, Quill.'

'You're telling me, sir! During Festival Week we have the devil of a job keeping them moving.'

'I see from my county membership card that the last match of the Stourminster Festival week, so called, ended on Tuesday the tenth of August!'

'Sir! If we knew that Mr Mallender was passing through Stourminster *then* and could make it stick!'

'I suggest, Quill, that you check with Major Burdett at county headquarters whether what Mallender rashly described did, in fact, happen at Stourminster. If so, I'm sure the major could give you the actual time: the catch may even have closed an innings.' Frank Fenwick described the incident. 'I remember, a fair time ago, there was a splendid Sikh who used to play in a turban. But nowadays, although one sees Indians and Pakistanis in county sides, I can think of only one regularly turbaned player . . .'

'Ah, sir!' said Quill, excited, 'you are thinking of our own—'

The telephone rang: Frank Fenwick excused himself and picked up the receiver. 'This is Stour Siblings 9184. Fenwick here. Yes, good morning. He is, certainly. Would you like to speak? Hold on a moment . . . Inspector Glover for you, Quill. Take my chair.'

He returned to the room when he heard the ping of the bell. Quill was methodically putting away his notes. He looked up unsmilingly.

'Mr Fenwick, sir. They've found another body out in the Siblings. This time at Saint Osyth.'

XVIII

GOLDEN SUMMER in the Stour Siblings was nearly over. The unruffled acres, blindly pointing finger posts, low steeples and tree-lined brooks had been tarnished with violence, thought Quill as he drove on. A wonder they don't have those trees out and straighten the brooks, while they're about it: there soon won't be a branch or bush in sight. Wheat and barley, barley and wheat! The last time I was out here the land was crawling with yellow harvesters and thudding balers—'juggers', my child calls them.

'When we get to Saint Osyth, driver, make for the church. Mr Glover's incident office is in a red corrugated-iron hut by the side of the vicarage.'

Things were a little less forward here than they were well inland. When he came into the lee of the Thumbelow Drain, Quill noted that Mr Coleman of Fullers still had his baled straw to carry. But a tractor fitted with hydraulic lifter, was already tittuping along with load aloft. Ah, well, Mr Chew would soon be saying that all was safely gathered in: that is, if he could take his mind off the art-grabs and murders in his parish.

As they slowed down near the vicarage, a flurry of sparrows rose from the stubble fields opposite the Wellingtonias. He gloomily noted that police vans had been drawn up against the village room and that a woman p.c. was clearing an outside drain blocked with tea-leaves. A refuse bin had not been emptied; and there was a scatter of dog-eared, out-dated comics.

Within, however, the place was in good order. His spirits rose at the signs of purposeful activity. The diary of events was set out; and he got down to the paper work.

It seemed that two small boys, Micky aged eight and Nicky aged six, grandchildren of a Mrs Wintle, aged fifty-seven of number three Pit Cottages, had been sent by her that morning at approximately 07.30 hrs 'to take a look at vicarage lane'. They had been joined by a friendly dog as they were walking in the Saint Sebastian direction. As they were about to pass the entrance to a field called the Pightle (map reference given), the dog had suddenly turned into it and made straight for some scattered straw bales. Under these the children had found a man's body, fully clothed. They had been frightened, and after ineffectually shouting, had run back to the vicarage. From there Mr Chew had telephoned the police, &c, &c . . .

When Inspector Glover joined him, they went to the little office that had been arranged behind the hessian curtains of a 'stage'.

'So he had been run over last night, Charles? But in a field. And we don't know who he may have been, or who-dunit? He was wearing a good-quality suit in light-weight tweed, grey shepherd's plaid pattern? Maker's name removed; but laundry mark on shirt and maker's name on hand-made shoes: London, West End? Nothing in his pockets excepting only three hundred pounds in fivers? No point at the moment in trying to guess what the money was for. We'll soon find out who he was. Have we any idea?'

'Yes, sir, a guess: Simmons, out there, thinks it might be an art-dealer, a Mr Mallender. He is going on the general look of the clothes. He once saw Mallender's back, he says. I thought we could get the girl from the gallery down here to identify. Simmons rather strenuously suggests that Sherard should be asked to do that.'

155

'We may have to get the girl if there is no one else suitable. There might be an objection to accepting Sherard's identification: I can think of no objection to *asking* him. We'll get him along. And the Jermyn Street bootmaker could undoubtedly interpret all that jiggery-pokery written in ink inside the shoe. We think it may have been an accident, eh?'

'Possible, yes. But then there has been an attempt to remove evidence of identity. Pretty feeble attempt. Delaying tactics, no more.'

'Hit and run driver?'

'It happened off the road, sir; and the body was moved later to be carelessly hidden. Furthermore, there's a mess of marks in the field entrance where the ground is soft; and some are quite recent: there were at least three vans there last night.'

'Ah, that's different. I'll take a look, Charles. Are you staying here?'

'I needn't, sir. Everyone has been. I think we should get the body away as soon as we can; and certainly before the school bus brings the kids home: we're having enough attention, as it is, from the grown-ups, if that's what they can be called.'

'Right, let's step along then. The vicar found you this place?'

'Yes. He offered us the vicarage at first. But they are about to go off on holiday: two Sunday-duties in Lincolnshire. He said he must be there by this weekend. I really don't see that we need delay him, sir?'

'No: we've got his statement. I'm afraid we haven't got either of his pictures back. This, as I recall, is the Pightle.'

The Pightle was separated from the road by a five-foot bank and hedge. There was no gate: just a wide gap: inside was a stack of four-inch field drains, some of which seemed to have been disturbed recently. About six yards further into the

156

field some screens had been set up round the victim of the 'accident'. As the Inspector had said, there were recent vehicle tracks where drivers had been turning off the road. Sergeant Simmons, in cloth cap and raincoat, and a uniformed constable from division were in attendance. So, at a remove, were certain residents. Simmons saluted. The spectators stared more intently. One of them even guffawed. A road (or 'length') man, with broom and shovel strapped to his bicycle cross-bar, had elected to join the crowd for his stint of 'work'. Snatches of talk, not all of it decorous, carried on the wind. The police were not unused to having a gallery.

'Everyone been and gone, I hear, Simmons,' said the Chief Superintendent.

'Sir! Doctor, photographs, casts, measurements.'

'I suggest, sir,' said the Inspector, 'that after the body has been moved, we wire off the area, including that stack of field drains. The beat officer says it has been there for a year or more. But you never know . . . About the deceased: if he had been stooping or kneeling close inside the hedge on either side of the entrance, he *could* have been accidentally knocked down by a car backing-in to turn; and that's what this heavy set of wheel-tracks suggests: in here; a sweep round the corner; out again, and off. I think he was run over on the edge of the stubble. He had been hit in the small of the back by something like a tail board; and then a big wheel went over his rib-cage. He was moved later: dragged further into the field, presumably when the identifying marks were cut from his clothing. Then these bales were dumped on top of him. There was an oily bit of printed rag under one of the bales. Perhaps from a farm tractor: perhaps not?'

'The farm men haven't been working here this week; and I agree that these three sets of tracks are quite fresh. The in-and-out hit-and-run lorry must have been a heavy brute.

It seems to have come and gone back in the Saint Osyth direction?'

'Yes, sir, six-wheeler, heavy duty tyres like those gravel lorries that have been going up and down here recently. This other, smaller one, with the distinct treads, crossed the exit tracks of the big fellow and went off in the opposite direction to Saint Seb: almost as if its driver had seen the whole thing and decided to get away from it quick?'

'He certainly left later, Charles; but how much later? He could have parked here early, come back on foot in the dark and just driven off. And so might number three. I suppose it's possible, though unlikely, that none had any connection with the others.'

'Number three had very worn treads. He could get in trouble from those if we catch him. Anyone round here, Constable, with tyres as worn as this?'

'Sir,' said the constable, coming to attention. 'I don't rightly know. We all knows they shouldn't be on the road, not really, with tyres as bald as this. But there might, none the less, be one or two about, doing errands, like, after dark.' He stood easy. Quill ruminated on Sibling breeds without the law.

'What's the story, Charles,' he said, 'about Micky and Nicky and their granny?'

'Mrs Wintle, sir,' said the Inspector, 'is never likely to miss the chance, as they say round here, to turn a turd to find a farthing.' The p.c. looked woodenly to his front. 'She's really a rather horrible old woman, known as "Ma Win" or "old lady Win".' He coughed, 'She wins things, all right. I had her statement,' he winced, 'in steamy squalor, while she boiled up unspeakable messes. Peering through her net curtains of late, she has seen the poor old vicar walking up and down, up and down between his gates and the Pightle, head bent, eyes on the road. "Reckon that'd lost suthick vallible". Early this morning Micky and Nicky were sent to see what they could find.'

Quill laughed. 'Who of late for cleanliness finds sixpence in his shoe? Although cleanliness is not perhaps a Wintle entitlement to rewards.'

'The vicar has had a lot to worry about.'

'Indeed he has. But I don't think the loss of the Rajah's Ruby need be added to them. Did the dog belong to the small boys?'

'No, sir. It's the vicarage dog, name of Tarquin. Very friendly animal which came bounding out of Mr Chew's garden to join the children.'

They were about to return to the incident office when they saw a woman p.c. approaching with some sense of importance. 'You had better see what it is, Charles.'

He did so. 'We've found a van like Mr Sherard's; only it's a plain dark blue. A telephone call from the Bestworths'. It had been driven into the water-splash by Saint Sebastian's church and holed itself on those stepping-stones.'

*　　*　　*

'I have no doubt at all: this is Rowland Mallender of the Cornford Gallery.' Sherard looked with distaste at what had been revealed of the body and at the bleak fittings of the mortuary. He twitched his nostrils. 'What unpleasant tasks you do contrive for me, Mr Quill.'

'Yes, sir. I'm sorry, but we're very grateful. Do you know the gentleman's next of kin?'

'I never heard of any. The whole of Mallender's provenance could be said to be obscure. He knew a lot of people in the gallery business, of course; and he had a partner who seldom came to London. I don't know where he lives, somewhere in Huntingdonshire, I believe, a youngish man, Lord Culvert.'

'It is not exactly cheerful in here, Mr Mallender. You could probably do with a cup of coffee. I hope you will let us run you back to London. But in the mean time would you mind if we shifted to my office in the next building?' When they had made this move Quill asked, 'Will deceased's secretary be available in Duke Street?'

'Judith Ramage? Nice girl: oh, I should certainly think so. She is used to coping on her own. But she will have to alert the noble lord and get him to shake off his sloth. For all our sakes I hope the business does not turn out to be in too much of a mess.'

'Do you think it has been run irregularly, sir?'

'I have no justification for suggesting any such thing, Chief Superintendent. But,' and he hesitated, 'I never found Mallender a straightforward sort of chap: he could never resist mystification. He doesn't owe me any money, by the way.'

'Oh, that's good. We shall probably put a man in to dig round; and we'll have to let the partner know. You have nothing definite in mind, then, about how the business was being run?'

'The Cornford have handled my work for some time. It's only in the last few years that Mallender has been in control. There are some Chancery Lane solicitors called Bema, Gradual and Terce. I had dealings with them in the early days; and I have heard Mallender speak to Mr Gradual once or twice on the telephone. I don't know how closely they were concerned with each other.'

Quill made a note of it. 'Now, sir, can you suggest why the late Mr Mallender should have been in these parts?'

'No, I can't; but I'm not wholly surprised. From some of his previous remarks, I got the impression that he knew something about the place.'

'It would be extremely helpful if you could remember

what he said, or the circumstances under which he spoke.'

'I suppose it must have been almost the last time that I saw him alive. I . . .'

'Excuse me, was it actually the last time?'

'No, that would have been at the private view of my Whitechapel show. I was thinking about a day last month, when I went up to London to see him.'

'Wednesday, the twenty-fifth, sir. As I remember, you went up on the Tuesday.'

'My goodness, Chief Superintendent, I don't remember as closely as all that! But I do remember that the vicar of the village next to Sebastian had just shown me my cousin's Vuillard, and I wanted Mallender's opinion.'

'You told us, sir, that you saw Mr Mallender on "picture business"; but you didn't tell us anything about the picture being the one we are all now looking for. If you had, it might have saved us a bit of bother.'

'Look here,' said Sherard with some impatience, 'the vicar said he was keeping an eye on it while my cousin was away. Well, I didn't know by then where my cousin had got to, or what he intended to do with the picture when he turned up again.'

'But you nevertheless told a London dealer all about it. Why?'

'I certainly didn't tell him "all about it". Having just seen this unforgettable picture for the second time in my life, I was particularly careful what I did say. If you understood the present-day art-market (and, by your leave, I'm assuming you don't) you would know that Mallender was very knowledgeable about where all the known Vuillards are to be found. Remember, please, that the first time I had seen this one had been under bombardment in Normandy. I was now reasonably sure that my cousin, acting on information I had myself given him during the war, had "won" this particular picture, but hadn't known how to dispose of it. This in spite of the fact that, when I met him after the war, he denied knowing what could have happened to it. Also we should remember that I would never have been shown it at Saint Osyth if my cousin had not disappeared. I can only assume that he had asked the vicar to give it house room because he realised that I was due at his own place and would be sure to recognise this Vuillard if I saw it.'

'If he didn't want you at the school-house, he need not have invited you?'

'Indeed, I don't know why he did ask me. But he'd had this picture rolled up so long he may have forgotten about it until he realised that I was due: the one person he didn't want to see it! Not that I would necessarily blame him for "liberating it", as we used to say. If anything I blamed him for bundling it about all this time without knowing how to cash in on it.'

'Which he could have done?'

'It's been known to happen, all right. Sometimes it is more difficult than others. If the original owner or members of his family had survived the war they could have started enquiries with Allied Military Government or something. That's why I thought of Mallender: he was just the sort of person to know if a picture like this had become "un-accounted-for", particularly since the origin of his own collection had been a mystery. When I described the picture carefully to Mallender, I distinctly got the impression that he already knew of its existence.'

'From your cousin?'

'Oh, I don't think so. It is unlikely that they knew each other. That is why I told Mallender that while I had been looking for "a" cousin, I had been shown this picture as belonging to him. I certainly did not tell Mallender *who* had shown it to me or where I had been at the time. He knew I had been out of London recently; but I did not even say in what part of the country I had been working.'

'Nothing to suggest Stourminster or the Siblings?'

'No. I am quite sure of that. But—'

'Yes, Mr Sherard?'

'I nevertheless got the impression that Mallender knew where I had been. Not, as I thought then, that it could matter. The only reason I refused to tell him everything is because his cocky mixture of caginess and curiosity annoyed me. As I think I told you, there were times when I wouldn't have trusted him in sight of a blind man's begging-bowl.'

There was a longish pause. Then Quill said, 'Mr Sherard, you think that Mr Mallender did not know your late cousin. I must now tell you that he and Thomas Pringle were frequently seen together at the Cornford Gallery. He didn't come to look at the exhibitions, it seems. He always went straight through to Mallender's own office. We don't know what they talked about. But in the light of what you have just told me, I would hazard a guess that they were cooking up ways to realise on the valuable picture that Thomas Pringle had been harbouring for so long.'

'For that matter, how long had my cousin known . . . ?'

'Known Mallender? We don't know. But we do know that for a short time five years ago Mallender lodged in the same house as Pringle in Chelsea. I gather that Mallender could have found ways of disposing of such a picture?'

'I certainly wouldn't put it past him. There could be risks . . .'

'Such as?'

'If Mallender had invented a story of how it came to be on the market, it would be less credible if the French owners had deposited information about it.'

'If they had not? If they themselves had not survived?'

'That would certainly make it much easier for Master Rowley.'

'He would know how to make sure?'

'It would have been just the thing that he was good at. Even so, it was a picture to attract attention. It would be reproduced in the magazines or even in some of the newspapers.'

'If the cover-story was fool-proof would it have mattered to your cousin or Mallender who heard it?'

'It wouldn't be fool-proof if I happened to be the fool who heard about it, Chief Superintendent.'

'Ah! You would have exposed it?'

'I am by no means sure what I would have done.'

'Nor would Mallender know how you might react?'

'I suppose not. He would have had a plan to cover that, I expect.'

'Mr Sherard, I have been indulging in some very unprofessional speculation. I didn't know this man. Was Mallender often hard up? Was he at all greedy?'

'I don't know how often he was in the red. Not the sort of thing I would spot. He has always been greedy: that's one thing he could never hide.'

'Ah! Instead of being content with a commission on sale, he might want the lot, with your cousin dead?'

'My God! Do you really think . . . ?'

'I am getting near to thinking that Mallender might have killed your cousin and that he knew exactly where he lived at Saint Sebastian. I think it was he who suggested that you be offered the school-house when you had to leave your London quarters. Has it occurred to you, sir, that if you could also have been got out of the way . . . ?'

'Do you mean that he planned to club us both?'

'I wasn't thinking on quite those lines. It would have been too crude a plan. If he had worked out how he could club your cousin in the church, he knew he would have to risk being seen sometime somewhere in the Stour Siblings. As a townsman he might think that a safe risk because he was totally unknown here. As it is, the mere rumour of his unknown van having been seen was a nine days' wonder.'

'Do you think he actually was down here?'

'We know that he was here on the evening that your cousin was killed. I was thinking, sir, that since Mr Mallender took pleasure in finishing things in a clever and complicated way, he might have been attracted by the idea of getting rid of you without risking his own further appearance or any further violence.'

'How could he do that, for heaven's sake?'

Quill told him.

XIX

'MISS JUDITH RAMAGE? I am Detective Inspector Glover of the Stourminster C.I.D. Good morning, miss: I believe you have already met Detective Sergeant Simmons?'

Miss Ramage, who had risen from her desk at the Cornford Gallery, sedately inclined her head. Simmons, who had come in a step behind the Inspector, greeted her with the merest flicker of an eyelid.

'We understand from an officer of this division,' continued the Inspector, while she, with a momentary flash of a dimple, sat down again, 'that you have agreed to help us with any questions that may arise concerning Mr Mallender's fatal accident. It is kind of you to have got here so early. A partner of your law firm, Messrs Bema, Gradual and Terce, is coming at ten o'clock.'

'Mr Gradual has already telephoned from Hampstead. He needed some more papers from his office.' She began to read from her telephone pad, and again there was a suggestion of the dimple. 'He sends his apologies that he cannot be here before ten-thirty and begs that you telephone his clerk at Chancery Lane if you wish to suggest some other arrangement. He also wishes to say, sir, that he is most distressed to learn of what has happened. He thought you should be—er— apprised of his ignorance of the gallery's policy, but that he deemed himself tolerably well equipped to discuss its financial position.' She looked up impassively. 'I expect you know that Mr Mallender's partner is not here at present?'

'We managed to speak to his housekeeper, Mrs Burton,

at—what is it?—Channel Cottage. She told us that she didn't know where he is or when he would be back.'

'We-ell, Mr Glover,' she smiled, 'that may be literally true: she hates parting with information. She used to be Lord Culvert's nanny, and "Mrs", by the way, is an honorary title. We often have to ask for news of his whereabouts and I cannot think Lord Culvert would mind your knowing where he is. Whether you can get him back is another matter. I hope you can: there will be a lot of decisions to be taken . . .'

'Will the business be in his hands, then?'

'The solicitors may be able to tell you that, Mr Glover.'

'Very good, miss. Do you get the impression that Lord Culvert was regularly consulted by Mr Mallender?'

'My "impression" is that the running was left entirely in Mr Mallender's hands.'

'Lord Culvert just put up the money?'

She thought about this. 'I really don't know. He isn't rich. Most of the estate was sold in his grandfather's time. Channel Cottage is really only a cottage. It used to be the agent's house. Lord Culvert is not married, you see, and spends a lot of time abroad. Our recent Biretta exhibition,' she smiled at Simmons, 'was his idea; and he is at present with a young Italian, Zuchetto, who is having some bronze-casting done at Verona. But I think they are both actually staying at Venice. I will find you the address of his usual hotel there.'

'Thank you, miss, we may need to get hold of him.'

'Can you tell me about Mr Mallender's accident, Mr Glover? I thought he was in Paris; but the police here said that he had been in a road accident in England—somewhere on the east coast.'

'It wasn't strictly speaking, on the road, miss. But it may have been an accident. He was run over in a field. We don't know why he was there; in the field, that is, or even what he was doing in the district. He seems to have been behind a hedge in a field which had bales of straw scattered about. The driver concerned tells us he saw no one, which is just possible. He decided he hadn't time to go where he'd intended, backed his heavy lorry into a field-entrance to turn, panicked when he found the going soft, thought he had bumped into a bale, slammed out of reverse and shot forward again. Mr Mallender's body was found next morning. The affair has a possible connection with another matter we are looking at.'

'Connected with Mr Mallender?'

'You said, miss, that you had expected Mr Mallender to be in France. Can you think why he should have been found near Stourminster?'

Should she have any idea? She looked for a moment at Simmons. But his expression was blank. 'I have no idea at all,' she said.

'Well, that's that,' said Glover. 'What do the gallery premises consist of?'

She rose. 'This is the exhibition-space. Mr Mallender usually leaves his own office open; but it's locked and he seems to have taken the key with him.'

'We have some of his keys: can you identify them?'

'Ah, yes. This is his office, this the mews entrance to our yard, this will be the basement back door. I don't know the others; but I would guess that this Yale is for his flat at Martingale Mansions.'

'We shall have to take charge of them. In the meantime . . .' He stiffened at sight of the 'stock' exhibition of prints that Simmons so well remembered helping to hang. 'Do you see what I see, Sergeant?'

'Yes, sir. Indeed, sir.'

A few had small red paper discs stuck on the corner of the glass.

'You've been here before, Sergeant. You said nothing about these red spots?'

'No, sir. I don't remember seeing them here, sir.'

'Bright red on a clean white ground. Showy, eh?'

Miss Ramage was firm. 'Mr Glover, I put one of these on whenever a work has been sold. I think this must be the first time Mr Simmons has been in the gallery after sales have been made.'

'Thank you, miss. We found one on the floor of Mr Mallender's van. Would that be normal?'

'Heavens, yes! He used the van for taking pictures about. These easily come off in handling. Sometimes when I get home I find one stuck to the sole of a shoe.'

'I see, miss, and thank you. They seem to be a sort of occupational hazard.'

* * *

Sure enough, they found another 'seal' sticky-side up on the linoleum of the picture-store in the basement. Glover smiled at Miss Ramage. She's a very pretty girl, he thought. No wonder Simmons seems a bit smitten. She came smartly to his aid; but she's too chic for him, poor fellow. He grinned at the box-files ranged above the picture racks.

He found the letter register where Simmons had made his find under 'Sherard'. Sure enough, also, the file to which it referred was not with the others. In the office upstairs, perhaps?

They passed into a dank scullery in the—according to Miss Ramage—augean basement. There was a wetly green area sprouting fern beyond the heavily barred window; and behind that a yard had been roofed with transparent corrugated sheeting which cast a yellowish light.

'What happens there?' he asked.

'Mr Mallender kept the van there; and there's a work-bench where he sometimes touched up frames and things.'

'He was a bit of a handy-man?'

'I think he was. He liked doing things out there after the gallery closed. He would sometimes distemper the screens we use; and early one morning I even saw him washing the car. I must say, that surprised me. I nipped upstairs before I was noticed.'

'Is that a blue van, rather tall and tapering?'

'That's it. Mr Sherard has one like it—different colour-scheme, of course.' She smiled.

'Yes, miss. We have heard of Mr Sherard's van. I think we've seen enough down here for the moment: the sergeant will give it a thorough go-over later. Can I take it that the whole of your accommodation comprises this yard and basement, the gallery upstairs and Mr Mallender's room at the back?'

'Certainly. The offices in the upper part of the house are nothing to do with us: they have their separate street entrance and stair. They belong to Investment Consultants or something ghastly.'

'And is the whole of the Cornford stock-in-trade here?'

'I couldn't say that, Mr Glover. I, myself, keep an up-to-date list of whatever is here, mainly so that I can answer telephone questions and find things quickly. But even so, I have no idea which belongs to the gallery. One-man shows and most new works artists leave with us are held on sale or return. Some of the really important pictures here we may only have a part share in. Of course, Mr Mallender knew how things stood. I try to keep track of what comes in and out so that I don't feel too much of a clot when he's away. Even so, I don't necessarily know what's in his office; and as for his flat at Martingale Mansions, I don't even know how big it is. He might have stacks of things there, including, perhaps, the two pictures you have been asking about. You see, even Lord Culvert sometimes takes things home, in the hope, I quote, of being able "to flog them round Huntingdonshire".'

'Well, miss, I had hoped for something more systematic.

Not that I'm blaming you. Your list, such as it is, may save us time if we can borrow it. But I think we had better see the room upstairs before Mr Gradual comes. Perhaps we can sit there and wait for him.'

'Certainly, Mr Glover. As I said, the door is normally left unlocked so that I can get in for any letters to file. And sometimes he carries off a whole file from down here. He often leaves one or two in his room or even takes them to his flat. Now that you have the key I shall be able to sort things out a bit. I don't expect you will find much of interest up there. It may be a bit stuffy having been shut up for so long.'

'Thank you, miss, shall we go and have a look?'

The office was a small room with a knee-hole desk, some comfortable-looking chairs and a short-legged upholstered object with a tall straight back, looking like a faldstool. The Inspector guessed that it would be for showing-off pictures to special customers. A couple of oil paintings in carved wood frames were leaning against a wall. Some box-files were on the floor by the desk.

The Inspector looked through these. One contained the Sherard correspondence. 'We'll borrow these, if you please, miss. The sergeant will give you a receipt for anything we take away.' There were some reference books which he took down one by one from a shelf, riffled through and replaced. He searched the desk-drawers rapidly but thoroughly. 'Nothing much here. We'll take this key-ring, Sergeant: six keys attached. Any idea, miss, what these would fit?'

She shook her head. She was beginning to look exhausted. 'If you will excuse me, sir. I think that may be Mr Gradual in the gallery.'

* * *

Glover had persuaded the lawyer to go with them to the flat in Martingale Mansions, leaving Miss Ramage to cope with what was left of the Cornford Gallery business. 'What will happen to that poor girl?' asked the Inspector while they were still in the police car. 'Will the other partner be able to cope?'

'She is a very capable young woman, Inspector. I don't know what will happen to the business. It is not a partnership, by the way. It's a limited company. There are two other shareholders besides Mallender and his lordship. It is Lord Culvert who is my client. We have always acted for the family; and I look after his interest in the Cornford business. Just as well, perhaps, um?'

'We have so far found no books, Mr Gradual.'

'Perhaps not, sir, perhaps not. They have not always been, um, easy to find. Mr Mallender used to do the book-keeping, and I shouldn't be surprised if he kept them in his flat, to which you are kindly taking me. They have always been properly audited, I may say.'

'Business steady and profitable, if I may ask?'

'You may ask, sir. Shall you be thinking of, um, putting a man in?'

'Like that, is it, Mr Gradual?'

'My very good sir,' he replied, with some coolness, 'my interest only touches his lordship. It is true that I originally advised him against a partnership. Quite so. His present holding is fortunately small, but he was able to make something on commission from time to time. You asked if the business were "steady and profitable"? Dear me, up and down, up and down. Profits from time to time have been high, very high indeed. But latterly, less so. This year we may even find that there is next to nothing in the kitty. I have always thought that the profitable ideas came from Mallender. Some of the young men Lord Culvert has wanted to back are very wild: not, um . . .'

'Not sound?'

'Dear me, no. Ah well! I hope to get his lordship away from Venice. As Arthur Hugh Clough so poetically put it,

> How light we move, how softly! Ah,
> Were life but as the gondola.

But life is not, um? I took the liberty of telephoning his lordship on a hint from the admirable Miss Ramage as to where I might reach him—We arrive? Goodness, gracious! Is this cliff of brick what you call Martingale Mansions, Inspector? Far, far from the Stones of Venice! After you, sir. It is your writ that will run in these, um, Mansions.'

They ascended by a steep flight of black and white tiled steps. Within the entrance they parleyed with someone in the porter's box, who emphasised the gravity of the situation by whispering, 'old police?' to the even more elderly-looking Mr Gradual. He confirmed that the key the Inspector held was, in fact, for the door of flat 532, belonging to a Mr Mallender, a very quiet bachelor-gentleman. Furnished tenancy, yes; but the cleaning lady said that the gentleman had one or two lovely things of his own. He then slowly took them to the fifth floor in a mahogany-panelled lift.

As the Inspector opened the door of 532 they saw a longish, well-lit passage containing a hat-stand, console-table, bentwood chair and numerous objects of art and virtu.

The porter reluctantly withdrew. Mr Gradual detained the Inspector by a touch. 'I should perhaps make it clear,' he said, 'before we enter this place, that my client's interest with the Cornford Galley consists only in the goods it sold or held by way of trade. I know that the late Mr Mallender used also to do similar business on his own account. This was no concern of Lord Culvert. Nor should Lord Culvert be held responsible for anything that . . .'

The Inspector interrupted him somewhat roughly, 'Yes? Well, well! Aha! That, for one, has no right to be here! I beg your pardon, sir.'

XX

GREGORY POLEYN and Frank Fenwick were fascinated by
the picture now leaning against the back of a chair in Chief
Superintendent Quill's office. Frank moved it slightly to
avoid awkward reflections from its surface.

'It would be rash for me,' said Mr Poleyn, 'to make an
unqualified identification. For one thing, it has been cleaned
quite recently; and heaven knows what touchings-up may
have taken place. But I really do believe that this is sub-
stantially the picture I knew when I was a young man. I even
remember the frame. Is it fair to ask if it fits the marks on
Saint Sebastian's wall?'

'In every way, sir.'

Poleyn rubbed his hands. 'Tell me, Mr Quill, have you,
ah, shown it to anyone?'

'Yes, we have. The experts agree that it has been recently
cleaned. The paint, they say, has been "rubbed" here and
there, and there are traces of "old yellow engrained varnish".
The re-applied varnish coat, however, is methacrylate, "a
resin",' he grinned, ' "quite unknown in the sixteenth
century".'

'And do they, ah, hazard a guess . . . ?'

'They say, sir, that "recent surface-disturbance pre-
cludes" what you yourself have referred to as unqualified
identification, Mr Poleyn.'

'Fiddlesticks, my dear sir! They can do better than that.
Have they the effrontery to tell us that acrylic resins were

unknown to sixteenth-century science and that *they* don't
know who painted this merely because some bright lad has
taken off a few centuries of candle smoke soot?'

'The artist is "Anon",' sir, 'of the "Cuzco School".'

'Cuzco? Aha! Peruvian Jesuits! Bernardo Bitti, perhaps?
I beg your pardon, Quill. It is just that I have been doing
some special reading since Canon Fenwick reminded me of
what I saw so long ago. In those days it was a black madonna
indeed. Probably plain dirty. It did not have this radiance.
Whoever cleaned it made a transformation—a revelation,
rather. I can now see four flying angels in the sky behind Our
Lady. And a cherub at her feet. Otherwise she stands, I see,
on a pedestal with strap-work edging. There are flowers in
vases at each side. Delightful! You have brought home a
beauty, Mr Quill. Bravo!'

'So say we all!' said Frank Fenwick. 'I am deeply moved
by its stillness. And yet all sorts of things are happening.
Bright harnessed angels descend like plummets. Flames blaze
in glory round our lady and even round the edge of the niche
she occupies. The Holy Child's cope and her own flicker
with radiance.

> The stars, with deep amaze
> Stand fix'd in steadfast gaze

on all these intricately worked patterns, on faces changing
from dark to fairest light. Nothing is out of place: all is
ranged in order serviceable.'

'Indeed, indeed!' crowed Mr Poleyn.

'Canon Fenwick, sir,' said Quill, 'I am to seek assurance
that the, er, picture be restored to the jurisdiction of the
archdeacon.'

Mr Poleyn bridled—almost sprang up.

'We have been helped,' Quill hastened to say, 'by a
partner of the legal firm of Bema, Gradual and Terce.'

'Aha!' said Frank Fenwick, 'The Triple Alliance of Chancery Lane, no less! They are an old-established firm, Poleyn, of ecclesiastical lawyers, whose spiritual home would have been the Court of Arches. I'm surprised to know they tangle with the police. Terce has a brother, of counsel, who is Chancellor of the diocese of Clunton and Clunbury. But they are quite correct, Quill. All that was in the church now comes under the jurisdiction of the archdeacon of Pars Magna.'

Mr Poleyn rose to take his leave. 'For whom, Mr Fenwick, you are a more than worthy Surrogate. I hope the venerable gentleman may realise how very fortunate he . . . Well, well, well, Mr Quill. I am reasonably sure that this beautiful picture is the Saint Sebastian madonna and child. If there are no further . . . ? Ah, you would like . . . Yes, that states my opinion very fairly and I agree to sign. Please do not bother to come with me. Ah, since you insist: you are very kind, my dear sir. I will leave you here, Mr Rural Dean. Congratulations! A very good day!'

On the Chief Superintendent's return, Frank said, 'Do tell me, Quill—that is if I may ask—was the unfortunate Pringle killed in the act of stealing this picture, which he had remembered from childhood to be in that church?'

'I am sure he was, sir, and by his accomplice.'

'Who was?'

'He and Mallender had been in collusion for some time. They planned to dispose of the picture we are now looking at, and also of the Vuillard you know about. But Mallender planned to take the whole of the proceeds. He came down one evening in his van. He left this in Mr Bestworth's drive while he and Pringle found their way into the church with Mallender's jemmy—broke and entered, in fact. Mallender's van is not only the same slightly unusual shape as Mr Sherard's, we think it may even have been roughly coloured to look like it. Mallender kept powder colours in the yard at Duke Street where he often mucked about in the evenings. His secretary even saw him washing the van early one morning last month.'

'This was the attempt to incriminate Sherard?'

'Oh, I think so; or part of the attempt, which may have begun as a possible second line of defence; but if he could have got Mr Sherard out of the way for a good long stretch, he would have been able to operate more freely in disposing of the French picture.'

'Which he knew Pringle had his hands on?'

'We think it was the disposal of this which led Pringle to consult with Mallender in the first place. Sherard would have been the one person they neither of them wanted to know what was going on.'

'Surely Pringle would not consent to any scheme to incriminate his cousin.'

'I don't suppose he was aware of it. When Pringle came into his father's money he retired to childhood haunts. He got thoroughly bored, toyed with the idea of opening a shop, but was plagued with the knowledge that he was sitting on this potentially valuable but useless object. He may even have moved from London to lessen the chance of his cousin seeing it.'

'But you think he had discussed this problem with Mallender? Went up to London to see the little man of the Cornford Gallery, his cousin's own dealer?'

'We know that Pringle had met Mallender before he left London. They were even for a time in the same lodging-house in Chelsea. Whether Pringle had started to unburden himself there we cannot know. Mallender may have seemed a natural person to turn to later. We know that Pringle at one time visited him at the gallery.'

'So you think Mallender worked out a scheme for selling

the picture without involving Sherard, and then, for his own purposes, saw how he could work it out even better *by* involving Sherard? Vainglorious and wicked pride, eh, Quill?'

'Yes, sir. His plan became more elaborate as he saw further and further possibilities. "Look," he says to silly, greedy, Pringle, "your famous cousin has got this important show and he is being turned out of his studio. Offer him your place for a month: that will get him away from the London art-scene, where he always seems to know what is going on. Then you can bring me your picture. I know someone who will buy it and ask no questions. We go fifty-fifty, eh?" "Oh, thank you, Mr Mallender! And do you know, there's a church in my village that has been derelict for years, with a strange old picture that nobody knows about: it's behind some panelling. Do you think we could sell that too?" And he describes it. Mallender says, "Certainly. I'll nip down one evening and have a dekko. Leave it all to me. I'll let you know when to expect me . . ." '

'Dilly, dilly, dilly. Need Pringle have come to be killed?'

'Well, sir. Pringle's death would have advantages for Mallender, who could collect all the money and not share a penny of it. Also if Pringle's death could be made to incriminate Sherard, Mallender would be left with a clear field to work in.'

'Yes, Quill, that's horribly plausible. But is there any actual evidence that Mallender was in the church?'

'Oh, yes, sir. After we found Mallender's body we found his van, which had been ditched opposite Parflete.'

Frank winced. 'How did the van get itself to the house with the silly name?'

'He'd had it with him, all right, in the Pightle at Saint Osyth. We've yet to find who ditched it later. The tyre marks are distinct. It was Mallender's licence number. The tailor's tab cut from his suit together with his keys and a pocket diary were found all together in a twist of oily rag that someone had rammed into the glove pocket. One of those art-gallery red paper seals was on the floor. Even a jemmy with his prints was in the boot.'

'Yes, well,' said Frank, wrinkling his nose, 'if all this was planted outside the church in September does it tell us that Mallender, lying dead in the next hamlet killed Thomas Pringle at Saint Seb in August?'

'Well, sir. You will remember what we then found. We now find that Mallender's shoes fit the tracks accompanying Pringle's in the church; and his cotton gloves match the mark of the small hand on the wall from which this picture was taken. It's a torn glove, with a hole over the index finger and a slit down the side of the thumb.'

'Right, Quill. If Mallender broke in with Pringle, he seems to have cut it a bit fine before Sherard's expected arrival in the village.'

'Well, sir, his determination to use the precious six-year-old note might account for his time-table.'

'You remember, Quill, that Pringle never got this note: it was planted on him posthumously. But I see your point: it was solely used to incriminate Sherard. Do we conclude that the letter Sherard really sent confirming his intended Thursday arrival made Pringle lose his head, so that he dashed off to Saint Osyth with the Vuillard and begged the vicar to look after it for a day or so?'

'Yes, sir. That's about it. He would have counted on being able to collect it from the vicar on his way up to London after he had seen his cousin established at Saint Seb.'

'But before Sherard actually arrived on Thursday, Mallender had come down surreptitiously on Tuesday to collect both pictures. And he had intended, if he got half a chance, to leave a dead Pringle, as it were on Sherard's doorstep?'

'Indeed. Half his plan went through. He killed Pringle, collected the madonna, temporarily re-parked under a tree near the deserted Green, and let himself into Pringle's place to hunt for the other picture. Even so he took a frightful risk of being seen.'

'His van *was* seen, Quill. But from the way he had camouflaged it, the fact helped his plan to deflect attention towards Sherard. However, he found no Vuillard . . .'

'No, sir. Mr Sherard says that "someone" must have searched Pringle's place: he has described the way it had been left.'

'Mallender had certainly been unable to ask Pringle where the Vuillard had got to.'

'He'd had to go home almost empty-handed.'

'He went home red-handed, Quill. What happened next?'

'Mr Sherard, of all people, turned up to see him two weeks later with the news that he had been shown this Vuillard picture only the day before.'

'But Sherard didn't say where he'd seen it. However, in spite of his caginess I expect he gave away far more than he intended. What would have been Mallender's next move, Quill?'

'So far, I can only make a guess. Would you mind, sir, if I talk it over with you?'

XXI

'I SEE, PENELOPE, that Meg Capper has now made an honest man of her poor old boy.'

'They're married at last? How horrible! My dear Frank, where on earth did you see it?'

'You may well ask. Not in "The Times". It was an almost furtive affair: certainly no theatrical garden party.' He handed her a copy of the lunch-time edition of an evening paper. 'The chap says it was a registry-office wedding. Meg's dresser was the only guest. Not that I have anything against that after twenty years of touch and go, or whatever they've been playing at.'

'I must say, one wonders . . .'

'*Plus ça change* . . . ? Whatever change of heart or change of front they now intended, an unpublicised registry-office ceremony with one invitation can scarcely even be construed as a public social observance. What clichés can we think of to condone it?'

'Married before, in all but name?'

'They weren't in any respect: as for name, I can't see her changing that on playbills. We are being a bit unpleasant. We should rejoice that they have decided on closer links, eh, my dear?'

'Perhaps. Jack is not a patch on her.'

'Well, I expect she took the decision; and that's her affair. You agree that she would do the deciding?'

'Oh, I expect so.'

'You sound depressed, Penelope.'

'She's such a splendid creature, Frank. We seem to be landing her in for a sort of rescue operation: coming forward to "take him by the hand", as Trollope says. Not, as *you* say, that the gesture seems to have been exactly public.'

'Cheer up, my love. After twenty years, Meg has probably decided that she owes him more of herself than a *pied à terre* at Notting Hill. All these police questions may have prompted her to realise that she and Jack have always had something more to live for than their respective careers. She may have found their present position rather bleak, exposed and vulnerably extended. She gave the order to close ranks.'

'Do you think she felt threatened?'

'I shouldn't be surprised. Not so much threatened by the police as by premonitions of old age, or of being separated from a very old friend. The separation was a distinct possibility: Jack was at risk of being accused of robbery with violence.'

'My dear, do you mean killing his own cousin for the sake of a Cuzco altar-picture? Surely, that's absurd: it's not his kind of thing.'

'His cousin's Vuillard was very much his kind of thing, Penelope.'

'You didn't think anything of the sort?'

'No. And I sensed that both Quill and Glover knew that they hadn't enough against Jack to make it stick.'

She grimaced. 'That sounds as if they were trying to rig the evidence.'

'Nothing of the sort, my dear! They were being scrupulously fair. But at one time there was a *prima facie* case against Jack and against no one else.' He explained how this could be.

'And do you mean that the police might have made it "stick" if you hadn't queried that bogus note?'

'I don't think so. The other evidence was circumstantial and unsupported: Jack could have demolished it with an alibi; or, even without an alibi, a good lawyer could have shaken it to bits. And Quill knew it.'

'So Mallender need not have planted the bogus note at all?'

'Not only that, my dear. It was much too clever-clever a thing for him to have thought of. It actually back-fired; and in the end it led the police straight to Mallender's office.'

'My darling Frank, what a horrible man he was!'

'Oh, I think so. I didn't take to him; and I was un-doubtedly badly frightened to hear that he had been nosing after you within an hour of my having rumbled him as a murderer. He was talented, all right. But he was a kind of Lucifer.'

She put her hand on his arm. 'Frank, I don't like this at all. He deliberately destroyed a poor dim creature who had done him no harm. He then tried to get one of his own friends convicted of it.' She paused. 'He, he might even have tried to, to push you under a bus, or something.'

'That wouldn't have been clever enough for him, darling; although he did make the mistake of venting his venom. I expect he had never been able to keep his temper when talking to a taller man. But look, my love, shall we leave all this until after lunch? Let me pour you some sherry before the Chews arrive. You deserve it for agreeing to ask them at such short notice. Mrs Chew shall tell us about Lincolnshire; and I particularly want to explain to the vicar how the good Sergeant Simmons found the missing Vuillard.'

* * *

'This is excellent coffee, Mrs Fenwick, don't you agree, Martha?'

'Certainly, my dear,' said Mrs Chew. 'We had a very poor source of supply in the village where Martin was taking the duty. I didn't like to complain because we had been told that the woman who kept the shop was the only person who regularly attended mattins. I am sorry to learn, Canon, that it was the young gipsy, after all, who took that bit of picture. I can't understand what he saw in it. You say it is supposed to be quite valuable?'

'There's no doubt about it, Mrs Chew: a five-figure sum.'

'Think of that, Martha!' said Chew. Penelope thought of Hedda Gabler.

Mrs Chew was firm. 'Then that young man must have been put up to it!'

'Yes, Mrs Chew. That's not in question, either, I'm sorry to say. He had been quite carefully rehearsed by an un-scrupulous older man. He was to have made you an offer of between twenty and fifty new pence.'

'Fifty new pence, Mr Fenwick? But it wasn't for sale. I made that quite plain. It wasn't ours, you see.'

'I do understand that, Mrs Chew. This is where the young man began to exceed his instructions. He had been told, "in order to cover himself" to make out a list for you, with prices of every single thing he was able to buy. This was to have included, you see, "one odd length of canvas, part-painted". He knew, although he never understood why, that this worthless-seeming remnant was the real purpose of his calling on you at your vicarage.'

'I rather took to the young man,' she said.

'Yes, there's a lot that is attractive about him. It's sad, but he is at present in custody awaiting the Quarter Sessions. He asked to see me. He had already told his story to the police, and although it is not for me to comment at this stage I think you should know what happened to the picture in your attic.'

'Please, Canon.'

'When he found that it was not for sale he had run into a situation where he needed to improvise. His instructions had been, you see, to "buy" the canvas, roll it up carefully and destroy the bit of Essex board.'

'There was nothing wrong with the board: it was in excellent condition,' said Mr Chew.

'That's what he realised. He knew he could find a use for it if he removed the canvas. The canvas, in fact, promptly rolled itself up as he took out the tacks. So he left it lying in a corner and took the board down with him to his van. He loaded your other stuff on top of it and returned to the attic for something he had forgotten.'

'That's right, Mr Fenwick. He came to the back door and gave me the money for what he had bought. I checked, of course, by looking in the van. I suppose if I had seen that piece of plain board, I should have thought it part of the flooring of the van. I don't remember. Then he said he'd left the list upstairs which he wanted to give me. I went back to my kitchen. He came down with it almost at once.'

'He says he had been supplied with this duplicate-book and wasn't used to such things. However, as he was finally leaving your attic he saw this tight roll of canvas and threw it out of the window to where his van was standing.'

'So this *really* was what he had been sent to get?'

'Exactly, Chew. He thought he would "borrow" it, pending fresh instructions.'

' "Borrow"? ' snorted Mr Chew.

'So the poor boy took it after all,' said Mrs Chew.

'Well, he produced a sorry quibble about it. His actual words were, "In a manner of speaking I didn't take no picture. I hid that!" '

' "Hid it", Canon? In the garden? We searched high and low!'

'Of course you did, Chew. Mrs Chew, will you have some more coffee? Chew?'

'No more thank you. Well, my dear sir, if he didn't take it, he certainly didn't leave it behind.'

'I'm afraid he was quibbling.'

Mrs Chew said, 'Martin and I searched every—'

'Nook and cranny,' said her husband.

'It was in the Pightle,' said Frank.

'Think of that, Martha! Whatever would it be doing there? The ground's damp as often as not. Most unsuitable. I wouldn't . . .'

'Martin,' said his wife, 'we must be going. It was in the Pightle that Micky Wintle and his brother found that poor man.'

'To be sure, my dear. How very dreadful that was. And just as we were about to set forth on our holiday. We had hoped to take our minds off our other worry. It really was most un-*four*-chinnit.'

'This young Gotobed told the police, Chew, how that man was run over. He saw it happen.'

'How dreadful!' said Mrs Chew.

'Gotobed was in your Pightle, with the far-from-desirable character who had come to collect the picture, when a big six-wheel lorry drew up. When they realised it was only backing into the field to turn they remained hidden behind the hedge. Gotobed maintains that the ground was very bumpy and that with all the pitching about the driver would have had no idea what had happened before he drove off.'

'And is that likely, Canon? Dear me, Heaven knows we are used to these monsters clattering and bumping through the village; but I often wonder how much the drivers can know of what they may be doing . . . Poor fellow, what a thing to have . . . Did the police, um?'

'They knew the kind of vehicle and soon found the driver.

He is in trouble all round. It is not the first time he has had to admit to blinding on an unauthorised run. But the legal consequences for him might have been even more serious if it had not been for the evidence volunteered by this young Gotobed.'

'Volunteered?'

'Yes, Chew, I think I might say that. A Superintendent Brunskill, from another police division, pulled him in for questioning on a routine matter and found him in a very disturbed state. Gotobed insisted on telling this story. No doubt he realised that his having been on the spot might soon be established. But the Superintendent, who knows him well,* is convinced that in a good-natured, muddle-headed way, Gotobed was trying to exonerate the other driver.'

'Ah, that is good,' said Mrs Chew. 'Martin, we must certainly be off any moment.'

'Yes, my dear, certainly. Mrs Fenwick, I fear we have overstayed . . . a most excellent lunch, and a very kind thought at the time of our return to an empty, er, larder. You did not tell me, Canon, how that wretched daub had been hidden in my Pightle?'

'Ah, no. While the police were investigating the circumstances of this (as I think we must now say) accidental death, a detective sergeant noticed signs of recent disturbance in that stack of field drains. He found that a much longer row than usual had been laid end to end with the canvas inside. It was quite dry there, it seems.'

'Fancy that, Martha! Fancy that!'

* * *

'Well, really, Frank. We've let those poor people go without telling them the half of it.'

'What is it *you* want to know, my dear? The disreputable

Worse Than Death.

187

Mr Mallender seems to have been having a pee behind a hedge when it happened. I admit that I did not quite tell all. We did not want to keep them for ever. You gave us an excellent lunch; and she accepted his praise of your coffee with a good grace. I fancy there's washing-up for me to do, or are you expecting your Mrs thing?'

'You've left a whole ravel of loose ends, Frank. You didn't tell Mr Chew that the man killed on his glebe was one of the wickedest art dealers in England.'

Frank raised an eyebrow as he mentally ran through a list of runners-up for that bad eminence.

'Besides,' she continued, 'you didn't say that it was the man who had killed poor Mr Pringle. Mr Chew would want to know whodunit, surely?'

'I wasn't sure, my dear. I know that he and I found the body in one of his parish churches; but not killed by one of his parishioners. I am not being frivolous. He is not one to speculate concerning things over which he is no longer required to take action.'

'But really, Frank!'

'Is that not so, Penelope? He was far more worried over the loss of a picture entrusted to him. Now that the "wretched daub" has turned up he realises that there are other jobs enough awaiting him without his needing to chase art historians o'er moor and fen. As for Mrs Chew, after a womanly sigh for mischievous Charley Gotobed, she wants to get back to her parish and her poultry, all agog for chores and stores. And who shall blame her? The fact is, there are still things that you yourself want to hear, my love, even more than I do the welcome rattle of Mrs thing at the sink.'

'All right, Frank. Tell me what really happened in the Pightle, as everyone calls it. I haven't seen the word since I found it in *Lavengro* about the field someone wanted for a surreptitious prize fight.'

'Certainly. As I remember, that field belonged to a magistrate. Where were we? I suspect that Mrs thing has just broken a plate? No matter. It was late September dusk with no one else about, as Mallender and Gotobed supposed, when up came this Juggernaut. They froze. They may have winced: they should also have cried aloud, as it happened.'

'It was frightful, Frank!'

'Horrible! Mallender was dead—no doubt of it. If Charley Gotobed had just driven away he might not have been connected with the incident. But he started to look around. There was Mallender's car. Everyone locally knew that shape of van. His girl friend had even said that the first time she had seen it, by Saint Sebastian's church, she thought Charley might have been inside it. Everything about Mallender seemed to point to Charley, who was sick of being badgered over the whereabouts of the picture he had hidden. Let it stay hidden! Let Mallender stay hidden! He did not even take the money Mallender had brought. Just tried, in a panic, to hide his identity and to hide his body under straw.'

'What did he do with Mallender's van, Frank?'

'Bundled identifying details into an old bit of rag, shoved it into the van, and drove the van off to the place where the police would know it had first been sighted at Saint Seb. Literally ditched it there. He walked back to Saint Osyth for his own van.'

'It was then quite dark?'

'Oh, yes. He hadn't really been able to see what he was doing. Nor did he really know what he was up to. He did not take his van far. He had previously arranged to meet Mrs Tyler at Saint Osyth that coming day. He decided he would have to break things off for some time.'

'H'm!' said Penelope. 'Not very gallant!'

'No, my dear. Merely expedient. Another ditching

operation . . . Was that another breakage? No, I think she's only dropped the spoons.'

'What will happen to that young man, Frank?'

'I don't know, my dear. It's out of police hands. He's been accessary before and after a variety of facts. I think everyone will know that he was being manipulated by Mallender.'

'How did they come to know each other?'

'In an evil hour for him—indeed for everyone concerned. It was while Mallender was driving down to keep his appointment with the wretched Pringle. Mallender must already have been revolving elaborate plans to rob and murder. He had pulled in for petrol at that remote filling-station on the edge of Blake's Wood. While he was being served who should also turn up but Charley Gotobed? Charley tried to sell him an old mattress and volunteered a quotation for moving furniture in a hurry, and no questions asked.'

'Do you mean that he would accost a complete stranger with an offer to arrange a moonlight flit?'

'To keep his hand in, yes. They no doubt took stock of each other. "Any time, guv. Give us a tinkle at the Grimsby Hoy and leave a message for Charley G." It seems that later on, when Mallender needed to spy out the nakedness of Mrs Chew's attics, Charley G. and the telephone number of the Grimsby Hoy came in handy.'

Penelope groaned. 'What a horrible little man that picture dealer was, Frank. I wouldn't have minded so much if he had been small and round and rosy, rogue though he was. He was so meagre and sly and damp-looking. How did he know that Mr Chew should be involved, or where the Chews lived?'

'We don't know, of course. But it's fairly clear to me what would have happened after Jack Sherard had told him that the unsuspecting custodian of a Vuillard had just shown it to him and asked for news of the vanished owner.'

'I see, Frank. Did he know that Jack had been working at Saint Seb?'

'Indeed, he did: Mallender had virtually arranged it with the wretched cousin. Where, he would ask himself, in that bleak countryside would the wretched cousin have sought temporary custodianship for an unspecified work of art? The most obvious starting-point would be the local vicar. *Crockford* told him where the local vicarage could be found. He already knew where Charley could be found.'

'Could he rely on Charley spotting a Vuillard among broken bed-pans and stringless tennis rackets?'

' "A daubed canvas either tacked to a board or in a roll?" If anything of the sort was to be found, Charley was to buy it and everything else in the attic for sale. And Charley told me the assumed name which Mallender gave and the accommodation telephone number—also of a public house: Charley was to ask for "Jack S.".'

'What an unspeakable little man!' She was very angry.

'Well yes, my dear.' He looked tired. 'But really, you know, this means that once he'd started he was just drearily thorough. No turning back from a prize so well-worth planning and waiting for.'

'What do you suppose Jack will do with the Vuillard after all this?'

'Well, I expect the Tate might be interested. I know that the V. and A. are treating with the archdeacon for our Cuzco. But I rather think that Mr and Mrs Sherard will keep the Vuillard for themselves. So let us wish them well.'

Penelope was still simmering. 'Frank, I can't understand that horrible little man. Was he an Iago of sorts?'

'Oh, I don't think so. Basically I think he was just greedy. What was it Coleridge said about Iago? "Motive-hunting of motiveless malignity—how awful!" Master Rowley had no reason for hating Jack, unless it was that Jack was a tall fellow.'

'Darling, I hope he hasn't planted some motiveless time-bomb under you. His ghastly ingenuity led him to working up unjustifiable cases against completely innocent persons. Isn't there an American word for it? A frame? And I don't mean like picture-frame, although pictures seem to have come into it.'

'Yes, it was a "frame", all right. Do you know, I believe in eighteenth-century English the "sheriff's picture frame" meant the hangman's noose.'

Lynton Lamb is of course famous as an artist illustrator. When he turned, quite recently, to a very different field, and produced two highly successful detective stories—*Death of a Dissenter* and *Worse Than Death*—it was doubly surprising, to many of his readers, that he should have taken as his setting a remote East Anglian village, and as his detective a cricketing parson. It was all so far away from the art world. But now, in his third whodunit, he has brought off another coup, with a plot which links the rural pleasures of Fleury Feverel with the esoteric delights of the London galleries.

It all begins when one of the 'coming men', Jack Sherard, moves into the locality, using an abandoned church school as his studio. Or perhaps it begins when Mr Lamb's rector-detective, Frank Fenwick, is asked by his Archdeacon to take a look at the now disused church at St Sebastian Sibling; it's rumoured that a painting still hanging there may be of some value. Or perhaps the real beginning is when Fenwick pays his visit, and finds that the painting is missing and that there's a several-weeks-dead body under a pew.

For some time all the evidence dug up by the police—Mr Lamb's regulars, Quill and Glover, and their engaging young assistant, Sergeant Simmons—points in one direction. But Fenwick has strong doubts about the police case—some factors don't fit, and others fit too neatly. It takes the disappearance of another 'master-

[please turn to back flap

Jacket drawing by the author

£1.75

net.